The Reluctant First

Book One

—————

By

Ruairí Cinéad Ducantlin

Copyright

© 2021 by Ruairí Cinéad Ducantlin

All rights reserved. No part of this publication is available to be reproduced, stored in a retrieval system, or transmitted in any form, by any means, without the prior written permission of the author.

Disclaimer

This story is a work of fiction and is provided exclusively for entertainment purposes. This means everything written came from the author's imagination with the hope of entertaining you, the reader. Names, characters, businesses, places, events, and incidents are products of the author's imagination or used in a fictitious manner. Any resemblance to actual persons, living or dead, or actual events is entirely coincidental.

Table of Contents

Preface

Aðalborinn: An adjective of Icelandic origin. From the words Aðall which is "nobility" in English, and Borinn, which is "born" or "birth."

Pronounced correctly, the title is:
Ale-Bore-In.

Aðalborinn: Of Noble Birth

This chronicle began in Biomass with the attempt to exterminate six billion people. The clinical trials of the drug were designed to cure the common cold and flu. The new vaccine inadvertently created a group of metaphysically endowed humans. At first, no one fully understood the extent of their extraordinary abilities.

Aalborinn continues the story of The Redeemer, the most powerful of the enhanced humans. Ten years after the defeat of the Muh'xan, the full breadth of The Redeemer's daughter's powers emerge.

Fear not, dear reader, this story stands alone. Aalborinn begins a new chronicle of growth, redemption, and overcoming the shadow of being the daughter of The Redeemer.

This writing does not follow the conventional structure for novels of fantasy and adventure. The structure of this story is a design that will evoke imagery and scene context. The style of this tale is somewhere between a Science Fiction/Fantasy Novel and a Television Screenplay.

Please, read on, immerse yourself in the descriptions. Consider the implications of possessing unlimited strength of will.

Or not.

It is, as always, your choice.

The legend of Aalborinn begins now.

Prologue

*"Our greatest glory is not in never falling,
but in rising every time we fall."*
Confucius

Ten years. A decade. That is how long Earth has been at peace with the interstellar capable inhabitants in the place humans refer to as the Orion Spur of the Milky Way Galaxy.

Ten glorious years.

Of course, there was the occasional assassination attempt. Some want my friend Corb, The Redeemer, dead. Top of the enemies list are the Xjaal. But they will be gone soon. We destroyed their cloning factories, and the Ajawlil warrior clones ensure the destroyed Xjaal factories stay offline.

The Ajawlil enjoy their newfound power and authority. Their loyalty to The Redeemer has not wavered.

Ajawlil warriors swear allegiance to defend The Redeemer, but the Plentari are Earth's closest allies, and they revere The Redeemer. He did, after all, save their species.

A warning to the reader, Plentari is an irregular word in English. Based on context, it is a noun that is singular or plural. Plentari is the name of a solar system, a planet, and the planet's inhabitants.

The Ch'en are another story. Once powerful

and influential, their repeated failed attempts to control The Redeemer have isolated the residents of K'an. They suffer from the imposed isolation and lack of trade. The coveted 'harmony' of the Ch'en society has been sorely tested under the unwritten galactic agreement to isolate the schemers and grifters.

There are other intelligent species with which humans have contact, but this story is not about those who chose to stand on the side and watch the galaxy evolve.

Aalborinn is a tale of being born not into a noble family but of being born with nobility.

Aalborinn is the story of Corb's daughter, Bonnie.

Aboard the starship, the *Dugr*, the first shift is on the bridge. Comprised of Lucinda, Ragnar, Nick, Corb, Janish, NT, and Landry, the crew has been flying together for almost three decades. With over a decade lost to the time-dilation effect of extended space travel, the team is physically younger than their given age.

Technically, Landry is everywhere, all the time, and is designated an Artificial Person.

In reality, Landry is a light green three-hundred-centimeter cube mounted to the wall of the *Dugr*'s communications office. He appears to the crew as an avatar. Usually, between one and three feet tall, Landry has taken on his avatar's responsibility to appear in context.

When he appears on the bridge, he is wearing a Celestial Council uniform. When he appears in the galley, he is wearing casual clothes. In the medical bay, scrubs and a white coat. In the engine room or the main hold, fatigues.

Created by the original Overlords, also known as The First, Landry, and Jol, are the only Artificial Persons in the galaxy. Jol works with the Earth's Celestial Council from the space station in geosynchronous orbit over Geneva.

The *Dugr* is a unique spacecraft and is named using an old Norse word, which translates to *Fearless*. Fast enough to be an attack fighter but big enough to be a small carrier. Powerful enough to stand and fight, the *Dugr* is primarily an exploration vessel.

It is a good thing we took the Data Pods from the Xjaal before we blew away the Xjaal council building. The Data Pods possess the records we needed to understand the accumulation of technology we found on Rýma, where we acquired the *Dugr*.

Fast, powerful, perhaps the *Dugr*'s stealth mode has been the most useful tool.

Hiding is a good use of the stealth mode.

Landry helps control the big ship, but his algorithms do not permit him to pilot the *Dugr* or fire weapons. The human crew is required to operate the vessel or engage in battle.

Lucinda Louise Raitt is the *Dugr*'s captain. A Canadian, she was a full Colonel reporting to the Celestial Council before she, Ragnar, and Nick resigned their commissions.

The Terra Carina Celestial Council, the TC3, is Earth's governing body for all space and interstellar-related activities. The TC3 is said to disavow knowledge of the current mission, but everyone knows nothing happens related to interstellar activities without a sanction from the TC3.

Lucinda is bonded to me, Nathan Tiberius (NT) Brooks. I am the *Dugr*'s Maintenance Chief. More importantly, I am the person who uncovered and exposed the original plot to kill six billion people. I joined Lucinda's counter-terrorism team to prevent the distribution of the genocide agent, Coldstar. We conducted successful raids in Dallas and Waxahachie, Texas. What we did not know until later was the astonishing part. The new drug's clinical trials, designed to cure the common cold and flu, inadvertently created a faction of metaphysically endowed humans. At first, no one fully understood the extent of their extraordinary abilities, the Summitate powers. With Corb's help, using his powers, we eventually learned how to control the new skills.

Corb learned to control the new abilities.
We watched.

Eventually, the egg-heads studying the new powers created three categories:

Those with the Summitate Potentia have the power to move objects. A form of telekinesis and teleportation, as long as they hold their breath, they can transport themselves to almost anywhere.

The Summitate Medicina-Aspicios have both the ability to heal wounds and to perform a form of remote viewing.

The Summitate Rationalis enjoy increased mental abilities. The gift of Summitate Rationalis improves the ability to think in a coherent approach, with superior cognition, and at a remarkable speed.

Corb is the only human known to possess and control all three abilities. Managing the new skills led to Earth gaining the technology for interstellar travel.

Ragnar Olaf Jensen, who is Norwegian, was a Lieutenant Colonel also assigned to the TC3. The *Dugr*'s Executive Officer, the XO, is also one of the original counter-terrorism taskforce members. He is married to Cassandra (Cass) Brady, Ph.D. With her doctorate in Mesoamerican Studies, Cass is the ship's historian and resident intellectual.

Nicholas (Nick) Davies, who is British through-and-through, was a Major and had been on TC3's active reserve several years before the current mission. Originally Nick was the counter-terrorism taskforce's technical wizard. He turned his wizardry with computers into becoming the pilot for the *Jaguar* and *Dugr*. His significant other, Janish Anika Rao, agreed to retire and buy a little farm on a faraway piece of the British Isles. Janish is a technology whizz and the ship's Chief Science Officer. Do not let either of them fool you. Individually, they are computer wizards. Together, they are wicked scary smart.

Lucinda captains the ship with military precision.

Ragnar is never afraid to fire the weapons.

Nick flies the ship like it was built for aerial acrobatics.

It is their discipline and military strictness that has kept us alive on quite a few occasions. The critical point is the capacity that changed human history.

Janish, Lucinda, and Corb are the Triad.

Corb Levi Johnson is the reason we are all

here, in this ship, zipping through the trilateral domain.

Time for a sidebar. Let me explain the trilateral domain. The *Dugr* can enter into an advanced slipstream using the Triad's collective ability.

The normal slipstream is the slowest of the three methods of travel that are Faster-Than-Light, FTL. The *Dugr* and a few other starships are capable of initiating a slipstream.

Hyper-tunnels are bidirectional passageways between solar systems and are faster than the normal slipstream. Almost all interstellar travel is via the network of hyper-tunnels. The hyper-tunnels are faster but flawed: They have fixed entry and emergence points. Do you remember the assassination attempts I mentioned? The hyper-tunnel fixed entry and emergence points are perfect locations for an ambush.

There are also micro-wormholes. Mainly used for communications over long distances, in an emergency, a micro-wormhole can transport a person. Not just anyone can transport via a micro-wormhole. A person who can teleport can use the communications FTL path for transit by "jumping" into the micro-wormhole.

The several FTL methods of transport are slow when compared to the Triad using the advanced slipstream. Using the Triad's ability to push the *Dugr* into a parallel domain, the advanced slipstream becomes the trilateral domain. Not another reality or parallel dimension but not standard space.

The trilateral domain is unique.

Within the trilateral domain, the *Dugr* can travel faster than the quantum calculations say is possible. I recorded the process exactly how Corb explained it when he determined the Triad was the key to getting to and from Rýma.

"Enter the dark matter domain and pull a small piece of the dark energy domain in behind the ship. The opposing force accelerates the transit. When pulled forward, dark energy is similar to a wave on the ocean. Like a surfer, if you are paddling fast enough, you let the wave pick you up. You ride it and stay in front of the wave for as far as possible.

"Increase the amount of dark energy you pull behind you and you create a bigger wave. The bigger the wave, the faster you will transit through the dark matter conduit. A warning, though, it is harder to control a bigger wave and the resulting faster transit."

That description is the trilateral domain boiled down.

The *Dugr*'s design parameters are specific to travel using the Triad and the trilateral domain. Lucinda, Janish, and Corb sit in the three seats on the bridge's triangular riser. From the riser, the

Triad controls the trilateral domain slipstream. Connected to the symbols embedded on the triangular riser, the *Dugr* is the only known ship capable of the super-speedy FTL transit.

As I mentioned, it was Corb who learned to control the Summitate powers. It was Corb who found the Mayan Shaman, who led him to the interstellar portal under the Xunantunich temple in Belize. The other end of the interstellar portal is the Planet K'an and the Ch'en people. It was the Ch'en who induced Earth's technological leap into becoming an interstellar capable species.

Corb's partner is Michelle Raye Wilbon. Michelle says her duties on Earth prevented her from joining the mission. The truth is, while Michelle loves Corb, she does not like space travel.

Together, they have one child, a daughter they named Georgina Levi Wilbon. Georgina, for the child's great-grandmother, her Nona. Levi, for her father. Wilbon, because of Michelle's fierce independence.

Born just before her father left for the mission that became known as the Muh'xan conquest, their daughter was eleven before meeting her father in person. Michelle sent Corb hundreds of video messages of his precocious child growing up.

Replying to one of the first messages, before

the *Dugr* went off the grid, Corb remarked to Michelle: "She's so lively and bubbly. She is a 'Bubbly Bunny.' Nick says his father would have called her a 'Bonnie Lass.'"

Corb watched his young daughter's video messages hundreds of times during the return from the hidden planet, Rýma, and the Muh'xan homeworld.

When she was about five years old, after hearing her father refer to her as a 'Bubbly Bunny' and a 'Bonnie Lass,' the child made an announcement.

"My name is Bonnie."

Michelle wanted to call her Georgie but was not surprised or saddened by the child's demand.

Everyone calls her Bonnie.

Part One

◆

Our Destiny: Simple Pleasures.

Dugr, Bridge

The first shift crew ignores the main monitors and the blue-green hue of the normal slipstream. Corb, Lucinda, and Janish occupy the riser's three seats. Only Cass appears busy. Her attention is bouncing between her console and her ever-present tablet while she tries to ignore Nick's persistent commentary.

"Cass, we don't know anything about these people. Are they ... people? Is this going to be a stand-up fight or another bug hunt?"

Cass ignored the Aliens movie reference. "Nick, you know better than that ... Of course, they are people. They are sentient."

"Whatever. Lucinda, why are we hell-bent on going to a place so far from civilization? We are so far out there if we get into trouble, there is no one close enough to help."

"Why are we going to the middle of nowhere? Because, Nick, like you, we volunteered."

"Yeah, it was a weak moment. Landry says six weeks to reach planet Megves Prime. Corb, do we have any idea what we are going to do when we get there?"

Corb ignores Nick's question. Nick continues to grumble.

"Fookin' 'ell, I shoulda stayed at home and

tended to the garden."

NT's follow-on verbal barb is on point.

"You mean tended to a few elbow exercises."

Ragnar fills the silence.

"If what I read is accurate, these people need a dose of The Redeemer."

The crew was surprised by the comment and the unusual phrasing from the stoic Norwegian. The crew gaze at Ragnar. Cass responded without looking up from her tablet.

"What Ragnar is saying is the lore and legends have nothing good to say about the people of Megves Prime. The Megvesnaith people are a special kind of evil. They make the Muh'xan look like Girl Scouts. Lucinda, should we proceed with the briefing?"

Lucinda closes the discussion.

"No, Cass, we will brief in the morning. Landry put up a clock."

Time to emergence: (43D) 07:12:11

Dugr, Bridge

The crew of the second shift has been on duty for ten of their twelve-hour rotation. Bonnie is sitting at Cass's duty station, to the right rear of the triangular riser. Reading mission summaries prepared by Cass, she is looking for any edge that may help the Megves system.

Bethany (Beth) Davies is Nick's niece. Ten years ago, she was a member of the first graduating class of the Terra Carina Celestial Academy, the TCCA. A British national, the RAF Captain also resigned her commission to join the mission and the crew of the *Dugr*. Sitting in the command chair, Beth loves being Lucinda's mentee.

Corey Michael Murphy is occupying Nick's navigation station. A recent graduate of the TCCA, the American Lieutenant agreed to the mission but refused to resign his commission. He remains active duty with the United States Air Force with a temporary duty assignment, a TDY, to the TC3. The TC3 placed the lieutenant on 'administrative leave' before allowing him to join the clandestine mission.

Always looking over his shoulder toward Bonnie, Beth takes a mental note to ask Bonnie about Corey.

Jirminach (JJ) Johnson is Plentari and is fealty bound to protect Corb. In the same TCCA class as Corey, JJ is the first Plentari to graduate from the TCCA.

JJ's mother, Jirmina, was the first Plentari to be fealty bound to protect Corb. Slight of build, standing five and one-half feet tall, the Plentari males appear frail and weak. Their blue-gray skin, short, stiff hair give the Plentari a sickly look to the human eye.

Looks can be deceiving.

Bored with inane banter, Bonnie veers the conversation without looking up from her reading.

"Corey, the Megvesnaith people are as bad as the Muh'xan. No. They are worse."

"Worse? What is worse than ingesting living people into a primordial soup?"

Bonnie glances over her shoulder but does not respond. The word *ingesting* has triggered her memory of walking into the Plentari Military Academy and the feeling of being consumed. Of being swallowed by millennia of tradition and an overwhelming building. She is recalling her time attending the Plentari Military Academy.

A matriarchal society, the Plentari Military Academy is run by, and attended by, female Plentari. Bonnie was the first non-Plentari to enroll at the two-thousand-year-old warrior training facility.

Plentari, Training Academy

Six years ago, an Honor Guard was escorting eighteen-year-old Bonnie to the Plentari Military Academy entrance portal. In a society where males were wholly subservient until recently, the Honor Guard remains comprised of females. Wearing traditional Plentari battle gear, each of the guards carried a micro-laser saber and a staff. Their ranks and awards scarred into the left bicep and painted into their short hair.

To fit in, to not appear completely foreign, Bonnie has shaved her hair, all of it, to mimic the Plentari short fur. Her light-brown complexion stands out next to the blue-gray Plentari skin tones.

Off to her right, Bonnie sees a line of new trainees entering a smaller portal. The trainees are watching the foreigner and the honor guard.

They are my cohort.
They have sacrificed to be accepted by the academy.
They see me as privileged.

Approaching the academy's main entrance, the octagonal building walls appear to be growing out of the underlying bedrock. There are no windows or doors. The large portal is sealed by two panels, each panel three meters wide and five meters tall. No decorations. No titles or nameplates. No knobs, or buttons, or control panels.

Standing, surrounded by her honor guard, Bonnie knows this is a crucial moment. The guard captain turns and begins speaking. The universal translator was masking the Plentari's real voice.

Bonnie does not need a universal translator

to communicate with the Plentari. She interrupts.

"Captain, I understand your language. I do not need a translator."

Unphased, the captain continues.

"Daughter of The Redeemer, this is your moment. If you pass beyond this portal, you will select one of two choices. Do you understand?"

"Yes, captain."

"I ask again, Daughter of The Redeemer, do you understand?"

"Captain, I understand. Beyond the portal is either the path to the Plentari warrior way or there is death."

The honor guard disperses into a short gauntlet, six to a side, leading to the portal. The captain turns from Bonnie to the gauntlet then back to Bonnie.

"Daughter of The Redeemer, beyond the portal, and forever, you will be known as Aalborinn, Daughter of the Redeemer, First Daughter of the Plentari."

"If I return from the training."

"No, Enlightened One. Crossing the portal is enough."

Bonnie nods to the Captain before stepping forward. The honor guards begin striking their staffs on the stone pathway. Synchronized with Bonnie's steps, two strides from the massive portal, the panels dissipate and reappear after she crosses the threshold.

***Dugr*, Bridge**

Bonnie's focus returns to the present, her serious nature unchanged.

"Landry, how do I make a formal log entry?"

Landry's avatar appeared to the left of the main monitors.

"Miss Wilbon, state: Log Entry. Followed by your name. The title of what you are recording. Why you are recording, close with who is permitted to review the log entry. Log entries are capable of being created from anywhere on the ship. Usually, people make personal entries from the privacy of their cabin."

"Thank you. Log entry, Georgina Levi Wilbon, entry to confirm the change in my name and title. Classification: Public. Henceforth, I will be known as Aalborinn. Daughter of the Redeemer. First Daughter of the Plentari."

Bonnie ignores the raised eyebrows from Beth and Corey. She focuses on JJ, who comprehends the moment.

"It is true. You completed the training and accepted the name. The legends are never in error. You are truly Plentari."

Bonnie nods but does not respond to JJ's statement. She remembers a time at the training academy

Plentari, Training Academy

One rotation, one year in Earth terms, into her training, Bonnie is standing, looking across a desk at an older Plentari woman. The Plentari are a stern, joyless race. The woman across from Bonnie is fierce-looking and terrifying in her demeanor. Ashen blue-gray skin made more sallow under the shadow of graying fur. The color marks of rank and stature on her arm scars are faded. The diamond points of her fingernails less sharp. Her tunic is crisp and clean. She is older but has a distinct bearing and presence.

Bonnie is the only trainee granted the privilege of regular sessions with the academy's elusive counselor.

"Aalborinn, are we boring you with our traditions and training requirements? You have completed one rotation, but have you gained nothing? Have you read the legends? Does our training waste your time?"

"I have begun reading the legends. There are many. Counselor, I was considering my options."

"Options?"

"Yes, options. I have been thwarting abuse for one rotation. Every cycle, every day, a new battle. The undesirable comments are unending."

Mimicking her peer's voices and the

equivalent of Plentari being snide, Bonnie rattles off a series of insults.

"'She has 'no fur.' 'An honor guard for someone so weak?' 'She is the commandant's toy.' 'She receives special privileges from the counselor.' 'Without fur, she will not survive the training.'"

Back in the present, unblinking, Bonnie tells the Counselor her decision.

"I have considered many options. The requests for the Contest will not stop. Human values cannot keep me from becoming a Plentari Warrior. Only one choice matters. There is one path."

"I see ... What are some of the options for the trainee with 'no fur'? What is the path?"

Bonnie ignores the intentional attempt to get her to react. The Plentari hold their emotions close.

"Counselor, there is only one option."

"I believe you are correct. Are you worthy?"

"Counselor, I would not have come to Plentari, to this training, if I did not think I was worthy."

When the counselor nods, Bonnie departs and heads directly to the combat training floor.

This is the day.
Today, I will be Plentari.
It will stop today.

Show no fear.
Give no mercy.
Today, I will be Plentari.

Walking to the combat training area center, she hears the doors to the training floor close and the locks clank. Instinctively, she knows this is not the day she dies. She has seen her future in her Second Sight.

Today will be a day she does not easily forget.

Nine of the twenty-six Plentari warriors in Bonnie's training cohort encircle her. Seventeen are standing with their backs to the walls of the octagonal room.

Bonnie does not wait. Rubbing a wound that will be a scar on her forearm, she turns on her heel to face the Plentari, who used her diamond pointed fingernails to give Bonnie the gash. She steps toward the most feared of the trainees.

Jaderna.

Slightly taller. Stronger. Faster. All the trainees fear Jaderna. Jaderna's skin is flushed dark blue, indicating rage filling the Plentari. Bonnie has decided, for herself and the others, the abuse will stop.

Stop today.

Stop now.

Reaching up with her right hand, forming a C shape with her thumb and index finger, she is pointing the hand at Jaderna. Jaderna begins to choke. Jaderna's eight compadres step toward Bonnie.

Swinging her left hand in an arc, the eight attackers fly backward, tumbling across the floor.

Slowly, she arcs her right hand toward the floor. Jaderna is flailing but unable to breathe. Bonnie steps closer, towering over the prone fighter. The suffocating Plentari grabs Bonnie's left calf, digging in her razor-sharp nails. Bonnie ignores the pain and the blood, her left hand flicking away the Plentari's grip. Looking down, unblinking, she tells the other trainees their abuse will cease.

"My father was the first human to understand these powers. Do not mistake me for my father. I do not possess his kindness. Do not underestimate my resolve, as I will no longer suffer abuse. If you want to challenge me, request the Contest. None will be refused."

Bonnie's face was unemotional as the life drained from the Plentari under her telekinetic grip. When Jaderna had expired, Bonnie stood to her full five foot six before speaking softly. Slowly turning, looking at each of her classmates, she let them know she was not a weak human with no fur.

"I am Aalborinn, Daughter of the Redeemer, First Daughter of the Plentari. Anyone who doubts who I am, who doubts my resolve, may request the Contest. None will be refused."

Walking toward the doors, she hears the locks release before the doors slide open.

Dugr, Bridge

"JJ, it is true. I completed the training and accepted the title. I am Aalborinn, Daughter of the Redeemer, First Daughter of the Plentari."

Beth and Corey have been eyeing each other, trying to understand what is transpiring between JJ and Bonnie. Beth interjects. "Do we call you Aalborinn now?"

"If you want."

"Every Plentari name has a meaning. What does Aalborinn mean?"

Bonnie ignores Beth's question and turns back to her console. Beth persists. "Landry, what does the Plentari name Aalborinn mean?"

The avatar appeared, hovering off the deck, to Beth's right, between her command chair and Bonnie.

"The Plentari word Aalborinn is a name, and it is a title. It is a name rarely used and is sacred to the Plentari Core Beliefs. Also, it is a word whose English translation is: Of Noble Birth."

Everyone is staring at Bonnie's backside while she ignores the crew. Thinking, reminiscing, she refuses to look up.

Plentari, Training Academy

"Counselor, this is only year two. It is a constant battle. Someone is always picking a fight with the persistent requests for the Contest. Some days, two battles. They call it training. They request the Contest that they know they cannot win.

"I beat them all. I conquer every time. Killing Jaderna did not stop the abuse. Counselor, what do I do to stop the abuse? Do I start killing them? Kill them all? Counselor, what are the requirements of me?"

"No, Aalborinn, you do not need to kill them. You must make a change."

"A change?"

"Yes, a change. You know what you must do."

Bonnie had become comfortable with her new name. Aalborinn. Thinking, she understood her mentor was forcing her to say that which she refused to accept.

"I must beat them without my powers."
"That is correct."
"What if they kill me?"
"Do you possess the Second Sight?"
"Yes, but ..."
"Have you seen the future?"
"Yes."

"If you have seen the future, you ask an unworthy question."

Bonnie understands. Today's Contest will be different. Standing, nodding, she strides toward the training room. Stripping off her tunic while marching to the center of the octagonal room, she issues the challenge.

"Today is the day. Today we will battle. Today, I will not use my powers. The victor in this contest will not be because of noble birth. Today, the victor will be a Plentari warrior."

The twenty-one remaining trainees began stomping their feet in unison. They understood. Today was the day. Turning in a slow circle, eying each of her classmates, she stopped when Jadexna, younger sister of Jaderna, steps forward and drops her tunic.

All requests for the Contest are accepted. The battles waged, with most ending in a few minutes.

The battle of Bonnie and Jadexna is epic.

Each has hurt the other, and both are bleeding from facial cuts. Their bodies are bruised and battered. Bonnie is sure she has broken her nose and a couple of ribs. The wounds from Jadexna's diamond-shaped fingernails scream on her chest and back. Jadexna is balancing on one leg, her left arm hanging gingerly. Her left knee is swollen and unsteady. Blood from her facial cuts has dried and caked in the fine fur on her chest.

Growing up in Earth's one-G usually gives Bonnie a slight advantage in the point-seven-G of Plentari. Jadexna's strength and experience far out-weigh Bonnie's physical power.

Bonnie's hands and knuckles are screaming in pain. Repeatedly hitting a person in the face with your bare hands is painful.

Watching her foe circle, Bonnie knows the Plentari will not stop. She waits, anticipating the next attack. When it comes, Bonnie is ready.

The Plentari gathers her strength for the final charge. Rushing forward, her swollen eye misses the subtle clue.

Bonnie drops to one knee, grabs the attacker's right arm with her left hand. Arching back, her right hand reaches between the attacker's legs. She pulls and lifts, stands, and throws the attacker to the floor from overhead in one motion. The Plentari's head and shoulder hit the floor.

The foe is out cold.

A cheer erupts from the trainees: Aalborinn, Aalborinn, Aalborinn.

Willing herself to stand straight and tall, Bonnie leaves the training room for the infirmary.

Having learned to read the subtle face clues,

Bonnie can see the Plentari doctor is beaming from the examination table. Two trainees dump her opponent on to an adjacent exam bed.

"Do you need to check on Jadexna?"

"She is the loser. Winners are rewarded. That was a unique move."

"You saw the battle?"

"Yes, of course, everyone watched. Today was the day. Where did you learn that move? It is not taught here."

"Buffy the Vampire Slayer."

"What is Buffy the Vampire Slayer?"

"It is a television show about a girl who kills vampires."

"What is a vampire?"

"The Megvesnaith are vampires."

The Plentari doctor steps back. Usually, tolerant and brave, the doctor is visibly disturbed. Her bluish skin is turning pale and gray. Her fine fur is standing on end.

"That name is not permitted."

Bonnie nods in agreement allowing the doctor to step forward and continue stitching her face and setting the broken bones.

Dugr, Bridge

Bonnie's attention returns to Beth. "Yes,

that is what the name means: Of Noble Birth. At first, I thought they were just nice because of my father. Then I learned about their legends."

Uncharacteristically, JJ interrupts.

"You know?"

"Yes, JJ, I know about the legends."

Beth and Corey know something is transpiring between Bonnie and JJ, but they do not understand. Beth changes the subject.

"Landry?"

The artificial person's avatar appears, in its usual location, to the left front of the bridge. It materializes three feet off the deck and just to the left of the main monitors.

"Yes, Miss Davies?"

"Call me Beth. I thought the *Dugr* was a lot faster. The *Jaguar* was faster. I know about the Triad, the slipstream, and the opening of the trilateral domain. Why are we not using the riser?"

"Your supposition is correct. Using the trilateral domain is the fastest known transport method. The Triad can initiate the slipstream portal and ride the wave. However, controlling the trilateral wave is physically and mentally demanding. Using the portal for long periods requires a significant recovery period."

"I understand. I presume you performed the calculations confirming the *Dugr*'s FTL is superior to the hyper-tunnels?"

"Yes, the *Dugr* is capable of speeds well over

the hyper-tunnels. As you know, quantum calculations are challenging to confirm. However, the *Dugr* is somewhere between forty and eighty percent faster than the hyper-tunnels."

"Not to mention, there are no fixed entry and emergence points for the *Dugr*."

"That is correct, Mister Murphy. The most important calculation in using the *Dugr*'s FTL is ensuring the flight path does not intersect the gravitational field of a star. Or worse, the event horizon of a black hole."

While the discussion continues with the artificial person regarding their ability to quickly transit thousands of lightyears, Bonnie realizes the term "black hole" has pulled forward another memory from three years earlier.

Plentari, Training Academy

"Counselor, the Contests have ended. No one is willing to challenge the human who never loses."

"Aalborinn, that is a good thing. You can concentrate on your studies."

"Counselor, you know I do not need to study."

"I am aware of your knowledge. What is it you seek of me this day?"

"When I was a child, my Nona, my great-grandmother, told me a story. She said: 'One day, they will come for you. They know you possess the destiny to change history. When they come, will you be ready? When they come, they will call you into a long black hole. Do not hesitate. Go to the school on the faraway planet. You will learn many things. But never forget, never let it pass from your mind. They will come. When they come, you be ready.'"

"Your Nona's Second Sight was never wrong. What do you think it means?"

"Counselor, did you know my Nona?"

"No, I phrased the question incorrectly. What do you think it means, your Nona's warning?"

Instinctively, Bonnie knows the counselor is deflecting. "I always understood my Nona's warning to mean I would face assassins looking to pass revenge for something my father did, or did not, do. They will try to kill me to punish my father."

"That is not correct."

"Not correct? Which part?"

"The assassins will come. They are already here. What is not correct is their motive. They do not seek revenge on your father."

Bonnie sat, stone still, watching the unmoving form of her mentor. Thinking, it took several minutes for her to realize the truth of the message.

"They are coming to prevent me from doing something."

"That is the legend."

"Which legend?"

"I will tell you the legend of Aalborinn and the Seekers of Blood."

Dugr, Bridge

"BONNIE!"

"What, Beth? Sorry, I was thinking."

"We were saying we think the Triad should shorten our trip. Get close to the destination, but stop short. Let the Triad recuperate. What is the point of having a tool and not using it when needed? All these weeks in transit seem pointless to us."

"Okay, so ask them."

"We, uh ... We were, uh ..."

"You want me to ask my father?

"We thought it might be best."

Bonnie's attention fades again into memories of the academy.

Plentari, Training Academy

Bonnie is reading the Plentari legends. There are hundreds of stories, but only one with the word Aalborinn. She is rereading it when the door chimes.

"Enter."

"You have been summoned. You are to report to the second lecture space."

"Thank you. Do you know why I have been summoned? Do you know who else was summoned?"

"No and no. My instructions are to give you the message."

"Thank you again. I will arrive in a few moments."

The messenger turned and marched away from Bonnie's door. The rooms and corridors' octagonal shape meant the messenger was out of sight, around a corner, in a few strides.

I have never received a summons this late in the day.
This is it.

Reaching to pull on her combat vest and micro-laser saber, she stops and returns the vest to the rack but holds on to the saber.

I am Plentari.
I will fight as a Plentari.

Slipping off her tunic, bare-breasted, and wearing only the pantaloons required of all

trainees, Bonnie steps from her quarters toward
the designated lecture room.

> *They chose this room because of the*
> *dark corridor.*
> *'When they come, they will call you into*
> *a long black hole.'*
> *I can feel their hatred.*
> *Their connections are glowing.*
> *They are not in the corridor.*
> *They are in the room.*
> *The cameras are disabled.*
> *How is it I know all these things?*
> *Am I guessing?*
> *If I am guessing, and I am wrong, I will*
> *die.*
> *The doors.*
> *I understand.*
> *Someone is seated at the desk.*
> *The assassins will be behind me when I*
> *enter the room.*

Stopping short of the doors, Bonnie
recognizes what she must do to survive.

She begins to push open the doors but
allows them to close. The slight movement of the
doors pulls the assassins closer, ready to wield
their micro-laser sabers.

Bonnie telekinetically blasts the doors off
their hinges, slamming the assassins backward, off
their feet, knocked unconscious by the flying

doors. Stepping into the room, she points a hand at the unconscious assassins, snapping their necks.

Stepping further forward, Bonnie sees Jadexna is sitting at the desk. When the third assassin reaches for her micro-laser saber, Bonnie telekinetically slams the Plentari's hand down on the desktop. Continuing the pressure, she is pinning the assassins' hand and micro-laser saber to the desktop.

"Tell me, Jadexna, should I kill you now or let the Madame Negotiator decide?"

"You are a fool. You are a human fool. You have no fur. The Madame Negotiator does not address the internal concerns of the Academy. If you were Plentari, you would know that."

"I am Plentari enough to know you are afraid. Your color has faded."

Enraged at the insult, Jadexna tries to stand and attack. Bonnie effortlessly pushes her foe back into the chair.

"You mistake me for my father. You think I possess his kindness. You believe his compassion is a weakness. His humanity is his power. You underestimate my power and my strength. My strength comes from one truth: I do not possess my father's kindness."

Using her left hand to keep Jadexna pressed into the chair, Bonnie walks around the desk. She collects the foe's micro-laser saber with her right hand.

"I will honor you as a Plentari. A quick death."

Before Jadexna could respond, her head toppled to the floor.

TC3, Head Office – Geneva

The chancellor of the Terra Carina Celestial Council, Michelle Wilbon, is seated at her desk. In her plush office, she receives news of the assassination attempt on her daughter.

Her response is matter-of-fact and unphased.

"Yes, I am aware."

"You know?"

"Yes."

"How did you know this just arrived."

Thinking, recalling a memory, Michelle does not respond. The Commander waits.

Nona's Backyard Gazebo

Michelle and her grandmother, Nona, are watching Michelle's daughter. Ten-year-old Bonnie is playing in the grass with a slew of toys. Nona is "holding court," educating the Wilbon women.

Curly-haired with skin the color of smooth caramel, Bonnie is always chatty, happy, and thoughtful. Her father says she is bubbly. He calls her his Bubbly Bunny. Never at a loss for an opinion, the child is a chatterbox. Michelle thinks they should put Bonnie's picture in the dictionary next to the word *precocious*. She loves the time Bonnie gets to spend with her Nona.

"Michelle, you know what I am telling you is a truth. You can try to change it, but you would have more success pushing back the sunrise."

"Do you know if Bonnie understands?"

"That child hears every word and knows things we have not yet begun to understand."

"What do you mean?"

"Bonnie, bring yourself to me."

The women watch the young'un scamper over to sit in her great-grandmother's lap. Michelle holds the gazebo swing steady with her foot. Nona is not as spry as she thinks. The young child in her lap is a touch too much for the frail octogenarian. Nonetheless, Nona's voice is firm, her eyes bright and crisp, her will unmatched.

"Bonnie, tell your mother what you told to me yesterday."

Turning to her mother, Bonnie is beaming. Shockingly articulate for someone so young, the Wilbon women are no longer surprised by the child's vocabulary, well-constructed sentences, or breadth and depth of understanding.

"Mother, before I complete my training, I

will be attacked. The attack will be unsuccessful. I will prepare for the attack. I must attend the training so that I may fully utilize the gifts."

"Gifts? You mean your Summitate Powers?"

"Yes, those and the others."

"Others?"

"Yes, there is more. Nona has seen it."

Looking from her child to her grandmother, Michelle receives a nod of confirmation from her Nona before turning back to her daughter. "Run and play."

When the young girl reaches the spot with her toys, she turns back to her elders.

"Mother, don't worry, Nona's Sight will pass to me before I depart for the training."

Michelle's head jerks back to her grandmother. Nona smiles and pats Michelle's arm.

TC3, Head Office

Michelle's focus returns to the present and the commander standing in front of her large desk.

"Commander ... My Nona ... Never mind.

"Next topic. Where are we with the builds?"

"The Garune tell us the ships will be ready in three months. Chancellor ..."

"Spit it out, Commander."

"Why don't we send a human advance team to supervise the builds?"

"How many times are you going to ask the

same question? Commander, I assure you, Chancellor Khatter was a lot more tolerant of your tedious nature. I will not continue to repeat myself."

Pausing, controlling her emotions, Michelle continues.

"Any other questions?"

The chastened Commander turns and leaves the opulent office. Michelle watches the doors close, thinking.

Every team we send comes back with a beat-up ship and half the crew we sent. Someone wants Earth to know The Redeemer is a target.

The large doors opening breaks Michelle's thoughts. "Speak of the devil, and who shows up?"

Chancellor Emeritus General Davinder Khatter and Michelle discuss the threats. They debate why they must agree to let Corb and the *Dugr* fly off to 'proactively' address a problem that does not yet exist.

"We have come a long way from Waxahachie. It is your show to run, Michelle ... Why did you let them talk you into the mission? Why send our most valuable asset on a mission with no support?"

"The *Dugr* will return."

"That ship is not our most valuable asset."

"Corb?"

"Yes, Corb. Also, why did you allow the old crew to tag along? This seems ... I know it is your show to run, but why?"

"Davinder, it was not a simple decision. What if I told you my Nona warned me, years ago, sending them was needed?"

"Nona? What did she tell you?"

"She told me there was going to come a time when I had to make a decision. A decision about life and death. What is more important, the lives of billions or my daughter's life?"

"Bonnie's life? What are you talking about?"

"First, you should know Lieutenant Murphy works for us as a TC3 operative. Lucinda is read-in on his mission and will not let him do anything stupid.

"Second, Beth is competent. She is going to become the captain of the *Dugr* when Lucinda retires.

Pausing, smiling, Michelle forces the impassive Davinder to smile.

"I am speaking as if this has already happened. Nona and her sight confuse things. Third, you would have done the same thing."

Staring down her mentor with a sly grin, Davinder had to admit the truth.

"Yes, I would have done the same thing, and you will do what is needed and make the right choices. You know the knives are going to be out

when you send them on the mission. The last time
we let them fly off, they did not return for eleven
years."

"True. But look at what they brought back.
By the way, I never took you for someone who
liked the mountains. You moved to West Virginia?"

"You know about that?"

"Of course, I know. Do you know who I am?"

They both laugh at the silly remark. TC3's
intelligence service is unrivaled.

"I like Q'eqchi. I like the people. I like
winter. I moved my family. You made the right
choice. If the rumors are true, the threat will be
big. We need to cut it off before it gains
momentum."

"Exactly my thinking. Enough talking. Let's
get some dinner. I want to hear about this ranch
you bought in West Virginia."

"It is not a ranch. Okay, maybe a small one."

Dugr, Bridge

Beth has become visibly disgusted with
Corey's constant questioning. Bonnie's attention is
on her console, but she is listening to the
argument.

"Corey, so what? Corb always comes home.
I was sitting in your seat when we took down the
Muh'xan. I know what it takes, I reject your

premise, and I reject your questions. I have put my faith in the people I know will succeed."

"Landry says there are too many unknowns. Do you think this is the best plan? I do not agree it is the best plan."

"If that is how you feel, why did you give up your commission to join Lucinda?"

Corey realizes he is verbally boxed into a corner. He deflects by turning to JJ.

"JJ, why did the Plentari adopt the human tradition of surnames? Taking family names?"

"It was decided to honor the gifts from humans by adding the additional name. When my mother sacrificed herself to destroy the Muh'xan, her children took the name Johnson."

"The family name of Corb, your father?"

"No, my father was from the area you call Scotland."

"Why the name Johnson?"

"To honor my mother. To honor her sacrifice and her loyalty to The Redeemer."

Bonnie's mind wanders back to when she learned her training had come to an end.

Plentari, Training Academy

"Madame Negotiator, we are honored by your presence. How may we help you?"

"Counselor, please gather the trainees. I have an announcement."

"They have already assembled. We received your advance notice. All is ready. Shall we?"

Plentari governance is a small group that is not elected. The few positions of authority are received when bequeathed along family lines. Heirs both blood and heirs chosen. The current Madame Negotiator is the first to break the bloodline in more than a thousand Earth years.

The Madame's entourage steps back, allowing the Academy Counselor and Commandant to walk in stride with the supreme Plentari leader.

They walk in silence, heading toward the Academy's main assembly hall, an octagonal replica of the Plentari Main Assembly hall.

The Madame Negotiator walks directly to the dais. Following millennia of tradition, the trainees, the instructors, and the entourage all bow. The traditional Plentari greeting is a slight bend at the waist, arms outstretched, palms up. The Madame negotiator returns the gesture.

"It is with great pleasure that I stand before you today. Trainees, the conclusion of the current training rotation is scheduled twenty-one cycles from this cycle. However, we have urgent need of your services. The current training rotation is complete as of this cycle.

"You have all been assigned a duty location. Some of you will be going off-world to support the

Plentari trade and commerce. Many will join the defense corps.

"A few will be asked to compete for a place in the royal guard. Before you refuse, know that we have removed the death requirement for those who fail the competition.

"Also, know we have augmented the royal guard training and selection processes. The training and selection processes now have challenges few will overcome.

"Finally, Aalborinn, Daughter of The Redeemer, First Daughter of the Plentari, please come forward."

Shocked at being called out by the most powerful Plentari, Bonnie's training kept her fear under control. Stepping forward, she stopped short of the dais before giving the bow of reverence.

The Madame Negotiator stepped off the dais to be on the same level as Bonnie. One of the Madame Negotiator's aides steps to their side, holding forward a small box. The aide opens the lid and stands still.

"I told your father and the many friends of the Plentari, there is much for the Plentari to learn. This is a new era. Today, we show the galaxy the Plentari have grown."

Reaching in the box, inserting the three fingers of her right hand, she pulls them out with the tips covered in three colors.

Bonnie senses what is coming. She drops her tunic, allowing it to bunch at her waist.

"You know our rituals?"

"Yes, Madame Negotiator, I have been trained well."

"Then, you know, this cannot be undone."

"Yes, Madame Negotiator."

Holding her hand and the colors high, in a loud voice meant to be a warning, the progressive Madame Negotiator changes Plentari history.

"Let it be known to all. Let anyone who challenges this know they are challenging the Plentari. We are one today, tomorrow, and forever. This person, a person with no fur, Aalborinn, Daughter of the Redeemer, is a Daughter of the Plentari."

Holding her hand high, turning to face everyone, the Madame Negotiator, in a single sweeping motion, from back to front, swipes Bonnie's left tricep and bicep. The diamond pointed fingernails diagonally cut three parallel lines on Bonnie's upper left arm. Ignoring the stinging from the colors seeping into the wounds, Bonnie stares straight ahead.

Wiping her hand, stepping back to the dais,

the Madame Negotiator issues surprising orders.

"Transport ships are arriving. Orders have been posted. Return to your quarters and make ready."

The Madame Negotiator stands still, watching the trainees filing out. When Bonnie reaches the exit, she is pulled out of line and directed back to the dais.

"Madame Negotiator?"

"Aalborinn, the *Dugr* is in orbit. You are to join them on a mission. Do not fail."

"The *Dugr*? The crew? My father?"

"Yes. The presence of the *Dugr* is known, but its mission is not known."

"I understand. I will get my gear and report to the transport."

"No need."

"Yes, I forgot. Thank you for your kindness."

"Creating history is not a kindness. It is a necessity."

"I take it as a kindness. Thank you."

Bonnie returned to her room to find her father, sitting at the desk, patiently waiting. After hugs, Bonnie begins packing. While packing her few belongings, Corb jumped to the heart of his presence.

"Hi, Bunny."

"Bunny ... I forgot how much I like you calling me that. They pushed-up graduation to get me out?"

Bonnie turns to remove her combat vest from the rack. Corb watches her gently pack it in its duffle. When she reaches for the micro-laser saber, he continues.

"Yes."

"Why? Did something important happen?"

"Yes, but let's wait until we are someplace more secure."

Eyeing her father sideways, she zipped the duffles before stepping over. Corb rose from the chair. She grabbed his elbow before teleporting. They both reappeared in the galley of the *Dugr*.

Cheers, cake, laughter, and too much beer followed.

Dugr, Bridge

"BONNIE!"

"Oh, damn. I am sorry. I was thinking."

"Yeah, we can tell. Are you all right?"

"I am fine, just distracted."

"Our shift is over. Landry has summoned us to the galley."

Time to emergence: (42D) 09:14:15

***Dugr*, Galley**

The crew had fallen into their familiar routine, a routine honed from years traveling in the *Jaguar* and the *Dugr*. They have assembled for breakfast. Nick stumbles along with his friendly but annoying banter.

"A week in, and it feels like old times. Ragnar, I know why you came. But ... Cass?"

"You are asking me why I left our daughter on Earth to join this adventure?"

"Well ... Ummm ... Yes."

"Nick, I miss Alva terribly. I am here for the same reason you are here. The same reason we are all here."

"Are you worried about the time dilation effect?"

"Yes, Janish, we are worried. My parents and Ragnar's parents have agreed to help. They understand what is required. Most importantly, Michelle has decided to help. No one knows more about waiting with a child for a parent to return than Michelle. Hopefully, this mission will end quickly. We will not miss too much of our child growing up. Besides ...

"She knows this is where we belong."

Nick tilts his coffee mug with acknowledgment.

Everyone turns to Corb, who looks up from

his bowl of Grapenuts.

"Powdered milk sucks. I forgot how much I hate it."

No one takes the bait, forcing Corb to continue.

"Landry, request the second shift report to the galley."

The avatar appears over the sideboard before they hear the response.

"Confirmed, the second shift is on their way to the galley."

When the second shift arrives, Beth and Corey grab a coffee before sitting at the long table. Lucinda waits for the second crew to settle before issuing the small order.

"Bonnie, Cass, you have a report on the Megvesnaith?"

Corey is visibly nervous, JJ is unreadable. Beth appears disinterested. Cass is looking over her tablet at Bonnie, who is oozing confidence but nods affirmative to the unspoken request. Cass begins the briefing.

"Planet Megves Prime is home to the Megvesnaith people. The Megvesnaith are capable of interstellar travel, but their system is so far out on the Orion spur, they do not engage in regular trade. They do, however, support an opportunistic system of trade."

Bonnie interrupts. "They charter and

commission pirates and slavers."

Cass presses forward. "That is correct, and the entire society is based on privateering. As far as we can tell, no other sentient species recognize their claim to the commissioning of raids and plundering.

"They get away with it because of their advanced technology. The Megvesnaith corsairs are the fastest known attack class ships. They outrun any ships sent in defense or to intercept their raiding parties."

Corey interrupts between bites of bagel. "They are not faster than *Dugr*. I thought a corsair was a pirate."

Cass rolls her eyes while looking over the top of her tablet. "A corsair is a term for a privateer or the privateer's ship. Continuing, they systematically raid and plunder other worlds. The Megvesnaith raid and plunder for two things: Technology and slaves. Female slaves."

Nick looks to Ragnar before interrupting Cass. "Something tells me these jamokes are not your ordinary pirate types."

Ragnar smiles, confirming Nick's assertion before he tilts his head to Cass. "As I was saying, technology and slaves. The Megvesnaith are an egalitarian society. Men and women rule and govern equally. Slaves, however, are almost always women and are used in every way possible.

"If that is not unpleasant enough for you,

ritual sacrifice is part of the Megvesnaith culture. It is their heritage."

Janish expresses disgust. "Ritual sacrifice, what does that mean, exactly?"

"Exactly what you think it means. Similar to the Aztecs and the Mayans, maiden slaves are presented for sacrifice to sustain the Megvesnaith cultural linages.

"Tall, pyramidal structures serve as alters. When volunteers are insufficient, slaves fill the gap. Primarily young maidens, but males are also sacrificed. Young boys are made eunuchs, trained in the rituals, then sacrificed to appease the gods."

"Bloody 'ell, it is Mesoamerica."

"Yes, Nick, precisely. But, and this is important, other Earth cultures performed human sacrifice. Numerous civilizations on Earth and hundreds of self-aware cultures across the Orion galactic arm practiced, and some still practice ritual sacrifice.

"We have come to understand, we believe anyway, the First, the Muh'xan, and the Megvesnaith had a symbiotic relationship. If the First built the *Dugr*, and there is no reason to think otherwise, they probably functioned in the role of facilitator for the Muh'xan and the Megvesnaith."

Corey has a hefty dose of disbelief and is unable to remain quiet. "You mean the First? The bastards who terrorized the galaxy before they died off. You are saying the First allowed the

Muh'xan and these Megvesnaith to assimilate and destroy entire populations as part of what ... an agreement?"

Cass turns on her professor's persona and teaches the student. "That is our working theory. It is a theory. If you have something better, we will listen.

"Well?

"I see. You want to challenge many years of study and analysis because you don't like the premise?"

"No. I am sorry. Please, continue."

Bonnie takes over the briefing. "As you know, this mission is a preemptive strike. What you do not know is why this mission is happening now. Why us? Dad?"

Corb looks around before his bright smile fades, and his crystal blue eyes grow focused and intense. "It is a simple problem with a complex solution. The Xjaal, before we eliminated their cloning facilities, played the long game. The Xjaal were confident the Muh'xan would succeed in destroying me, but they had a backup plan. Belts and suspenders."

Not yet understanding his role, Corey interrupts Corb's presentation.

"Belts and suspenders?"

Beth puts Corey in his place. "It means if you wear belts and suspenders, your pants won't fall. It is an analogy, maybe an allegory, for a safety net. Now, Lieutenant, please remain quiet until the briefing has completed."

Corb does not allow the chastened Lieutenant to respond. "The Xjaal's alternate plan is still in play. Landry, the map, please."

The video monitors morphed to an image of the Orion spur within the Milky Way Galaxy. Slowly zooming in, a red dot appeared at the right outer edge of the spur. A green dot appeared in the lower, center edge of the spur. Landry's avatar began the description. "The red dot represents the Megves system, the yellow dot the Sol system. The remaining dots, the other systems, are Earth's interstellar trading partners. The lines are a small portion of the hyper-tunnel network.

"As you can see, Sol is the closest system to Megves Prime, in a straight line. But there are no hyper-tunnels between the Megves system and Earth. The shortest route is this path."

Seven of the lines brightened, indicating the shortest path from Megves to Sol using the hyper-tunnels.

"The route is at least five months of travel in each direction."

"Hold up. You told us yesterday six weeks to Megves Prime."

"Correct, Nick, this is our flight path."

A direct line appeared from Sol to Megves. Corb finishes the briefing. "We believe there is a squadron of Megvesnaith attack cruisers and a transport ship headed to Sol. If the information is correct, we have three months to reach Megves Prime, correct the problem, and get back to Sol before the raiding force arrives."

Corey forgets the order to remain quiet. "Why didn't we ask for help, reinforce our defenses, and wait for the Megvesnaith to arrive? We could have destroyed the attackers and then dealt with the Megvesnaith homeworld."

Corb's tone remains even. "Because, Corey, our information indicates we are not capable of defeating a raiding squadron of Megvesnaith attack cruisers."

"You defeated the Xjaal and the Muh'xan. What is different about the Megvesnaith?"

Corb's eyebrow raised while he turned his head toward Cass. Cass ends her briefing. "Megvesnaith do not fight a battle with cannons and lasers. They deploy biologics that disable the population. If it requires a year of hit-and-run attacks to subdue the people, they will wait until they decimate the population before attacking and plundering.

"They are prepared to perform hundreds, thousands, of hit and run attacks to subdue the target. They do not bomb or nuke or fight ground battles with troops. They wear down their prey from space.

"It can take years. Eventually, the hit and run approach breaks the will of the prey. They give up, or they all die. Usually, the prey fights until they can fight no more. When they can fight no more, they surrender. The Megvesnaith wait for the surrender."

"Are you saying they raid entire planets for slaves?"

"Yes, Corey, raid entire planets is exactly what they do."

Cass presses a couple of icons before placing her dark tablet on the table. She unveils the truth of the Megvesnaith people. "The Megvesnaith are cannibalistic. The sick bastards harvest males for sustenance and enslave the females. Anyone not harvested or enslaved is left to rot. Now ... We think they are on course for Earth with a colonization force."

Death to All, Bridge

The Ajawlil clones are short, rail-thin, with a gray skin tone. Similar to, but smaller than, the Plentari, the Ajawlil arms hang just below the waistline. Three fingers and an opposable thumb terminate the thin arms. Led by Commodore Jexond, he is an outlier for their species. The commodore reaches a tall five-feet four-inches in height and weighs a staggering sixteen stone. At two-hundred and twenty-four pounds, the commodore outweighs any four Ajawlil.

Impressive in his purple and gold uniform,

the commodore commands all of the Ajawlil mercenary forces across the galaxy. The Commodore never leaves the Ajawlil flagship, the battlecruiser, *Death to All.*

"Commodore, I have confirmed the authenticity of the message."

"Very well, plot the course, begin the departure sequence. I will be in my ready room. Advise me when we reach the entrance to the hyper-tunnel."

"Yes, Commodore."

Dugr, Galley

The First shift has left the galley. Beth, Corey, and JJ are completing their end-of-shift meal and discussing the new information.

While JJ is silent, Corey is whining and complaining. Beth is unphased by the new information.

"So, what? Do you want to turn around and go home?"

"That is not what I am saying. Don't twist my words."

"What are your words? What are you saying?"

"I am saying we should have been told more about the mission before we agreed to join the crew."

"You know that is not how it works. There were hundreds of qualified applicants for your position. Why are you backing out now?"

"I am not backing out. I am just saying ... Never mind. JJ, what do the Plentari know of the Megvesnaith people?"

"Eating another? Ingesting blood? The Megvesnaith are not people."

Dugr, Bridge

The first shift has settled in for their rotation. Lucinda is tidying up minor personnel details.

"Bonnie, are you okay with splitting the shifts?"

"Lucinda, I do not mind the hours. I kind of like it. Last half of the second shift and the first half of the first shift. I do not mind. I am learning a lot."

"Good. Anything to report?"

"Yes, Beth will make a good captain."

Pleased, Lucinda closes the topic. "We all know that she has the skills. By report, I usually mean the status of the ship or something we don't know."

Nick changes the discussion tone. "We have known the mission parameters for three weeks. Enough is enough. Corb, I agree with Lucinda."

"Of course, you do. Nick, you have no patience. Janish, what about you?"

"I agree with Lucinda. We use the Triad, shorten this journey."

Corb responds by turning his chair to the center of the triangular riser. Lucinda and Janish do the same. The symbols on the riser begin to glow. Ragnar, Nick, NT, and Cass immediately reach for their protective goggles. Seeing the others, Bonnie dashes to the supply closet, pulling out eye protection and sitting down with a nod to Corb.

Lucinda turns on her captain's tone.

"Nick, drop us into real space."

The blue-green hue of the advanced slipstream conduit fades. A starfield replaces the blue-green shade. The vastness of space is evident.

"Landry?"

"Captain, we are very far from everywhere."

"I can see that. Plot a course. Nick, get us moving as soon as he has the course. I want entry at point-six the speed of light."

"Velocity, point-six *c*, confirmed."

The crew felt the *Dugr*'s big engines begin the process of moving the exploration/attack cruiser.

"Four minutes to speed."

"Thank you, Nick. Bonnie, you might want to ensure you have a blindfold under the goggles."

Looking around, Bonnie was unusually confused.

"Oh? What about these guys?"

"You are new. We all have nanobots that help us block the light."

"I see. Yes, I did not think of that. I will work with Landry to prepare a dose."

Corb stared at his daughter but remained quiet.

Time to entry: 00:01:01

Everyone re-positioned their goggles.

"Here we go people."

The riser symbols erupted with a bright white light.

Dugr, Bridge

Time to Megves: (29D) 17:21:51

"Landry, is that clock correct?"

"Yes, Lucinda, we were in the slipstream for just under twelve hours. We cut the transit time by approximately twenty percent using the trilateral slipstream."

"Landry, please request the second shift to report to the bridge. Janish, Corb?"

"I am fine, Lucinda, a little tired."

"Same."

"You are doing it wrong."

Everyone turned to Bonnie, who did not

leave the bridge at the end of her shift. Her eyes focused on her father. Corb returned the focus. "Would you care to elaborate?"

"You are using the power of all three. You are using the Triad to initiate and maintain the slipstream conduit. But you only need the Triad to initiate the conduit. After achieving velocity, one person can maintain the slipstream."

The bridge crew looked at each other, contemplating the implications of Bonnie's assertion. Beth, Corey, and JJ enter the bridge and stand to the side, waiting.

Corb understood what Bonnie had learned by observation of the Triad's connections. "It is simple Newtonian physics. It is Newton's first law. An object at rest stays at rest. An object in motion stays in motion, with the same speed and direction unless acted upon by an unbalanced force.

"We need the Triad to overcome the inertia and enter the trilateral domain. Once we are riding the wave, maintaining the velocity is a simple process of managing the momentum.

"I am surprised we did not see it sooner."

Turning to the newest member, the crew saw the young woman had her father's radiant smile.

"I was watching your connections. Did you know my father sleeps most of the time in the slipstream? No? I thought not. He does not know he is asleep. His connection does not lie."

Janish sounded like her husband, Nick. "Classic man, leave the women to do all the work."

Lucinda pulled the crew back to the topic. "Enough of this for now. We need to rest. Beth, I want you to supervise Bonnie and Landry. She is going to dose with nanites, the nanobots.

"Corey, get us back in the slipstream. Landry, check his flight calculations before he initiates."

Corey responds while taking Nick's vacated seat. "Confirmed, slipstream in ten minutes."

Landry's avatar chirps. "I got it, Lucinda. No flying through a star or into a black hole. The new guy will catch up."

Corey glares at the avatar before turning to the navigation console and begins pressing icons.

Dugr, Bridge

The first shift is ready for their rotation an hour early. Lucinda is standing in the portal, issuing orders.

"Beth, a report, please."

"Lucinda, nothing unusual. All systems report green."

"Thanks. Landry, have everyone report to the galley."

Lucinda turns toward the galley, the bridge portal doors closing behind her.

Dugr, Galley

Lucinda is in full captain mode. "If Bonnie is correct, we rotate the Triad. Landry, if we enter the slipstream conduit at point-six *c* and we do not stop to rest, how long before we reach the Megves system?"

"Approximately twenty-four to thirty hours."

"I am posting a new duty roster. After we are in the trilateral slipstream, initiate twelve-hour shifts for everyone except the Triad. We alternate duty stations on the twelve-hour cycle. We rotate the Triad on eight-hour shifts.

"Ragnar and JJ.

"Nick and Corey.

"Beth and NT.

"Cass and Bonnie.

"Corb, Janish, and I will rotate on eight-hour shifts to keep us in the trilateral domain.

"Questions?"

"Do we drop out early and reconnoiter the system?"

"Ragnar, excellent catch. Landry, do the math. I know quantum calculations and chaos theory is a best-guess. Blah, blah, blah. Give it your best effort."

"Confirmed, plot an emergence point two lightyears short of the Megves system."

"Any other questions?"

"Captain?"

"Corey, in the galley, we are informal. You may call me Lucinda. What is your question?"

"What are we going to do when we arrive?"

Corb intercepted the answer. "The mission brief will be on the other side of the transit. Landry, put up a clock."

Time to entry: 00:14:41
Time to emergence: 33:31:41

Dugr, Medical Bay

"Just a simple injection?"

"Yes, Bonnie, you don't even feel it."

"Cass, how long before you noticed they were helping?"

"For me, it took a couple of days. Janish and Lucinda said they felt the effects immediately. I guess everyone is different. Landry?"

Landry appears wearing a medical uniform.

"That's new."

"Yes, Cass, I decided it is better if I appear in a form closer to expected norms. I presume you are going to request confirmation of the medical procedure."

"You presume correctly. Is the dose correct?"

"Yes, the calculations are correct based on Miss Wilbon's body mass. However, you have chosen the older version of nanites. The current version is in the container, in Corb's cabin. Do you want me to request he bring the canister to the medical bay?"

"Yes, please."

Waiting, Cass and Bonnie eye each other. Cass returns the older nanites to their container.

Corb appears with a chrome canister. Placing it on the desk, he turns to Bonnie.

"You know this is not reversible, right? Once they are in your body, removal is impossible."

"I am aware. The nanites, under the right circumstances, could become sentient. What I do not understand is why you are not trying to talk me out of doing it?"

"I may be dumb, but I am not dumb enough to fight the wind."

Opening the chromium canister, Corb doles out the correct amount of nanites, by weight, before dropping them into the injector. Sealing the container, he turns to leave. "Remember, you control them. They don't control you."

Cass and Bonnie look at each other with confusion when the doors close behind Corb.

"You know my father better than I do. What the hell does that mean?"

"I have no idea. Pull up your sleeve. Let's get this over."

The injection is unnoticed. Bonnie feels immediate results. Her eyes morph in and out, briefly appearing digital, before returning to normal.

"It looks like you have control already?"

"Yes, they feel ... natural. As you said, everyone is different."

Dugr, Bridge

Time to emergence: 12:31:21

The riser symbols are glowing brightly. The beam from the center symbol is intense.

Lucinda is seated, monitoring the *Dugr's* momentum on the wave's crest in the trilateral slipstream.

"Cass, these nanobots are terrific. They are protecting my eyes. Just because I thought about it, they reacted."

"Yes, Bonnie, they are pretty amazing."

"I know why my father has kept them hidden."

"I am not sure hidden is the correct word. There are lots of things, information, and technologies that we have kept close. You know, all that need to know stuff."

"Do you think we are on the correct mission?"

"Do I think we are doing the right thing? Yes. You were an infant the last time we went off to fight a threat. You were eleven when we returned. These missions always seem poorly planned, fool-hearty, or plain dumb. The truth of it is they are still necessary.

"Don't ask me to explain it, but there is a level of trust required. Before my first mission, while your father and I were looking for clues under pyramids and in the desert, I would have said violence is never the correct path.

"Now ... I understand there are actions, some violent, that are for the greater good. Your father understood that before the rest of us accepted the premise.

"Why are you asking?"

"She is asking because this is her first mission."

"Ragnar, hush. Seriously, Bonnie, I do not think of you as a naïve rookie. Why are you asking?"

"Is it our responsibility to protect everyone, everywhere, from threats?"

"That is a good question. If helping others, defending others, helps Earth, does the end justify the means?"

"I suppose it does, but at what cost?"

"You are overthinking like a human. Not enough like a member of the greater collective of self-aware people. Human norms, your norms, do not apply to the rest of the galaxy.

"There is a little bit of the Wild West out here in space. Sometimes, the law is what you say it is if you are big enough and bad enough to enforce it."

"If it bleeds, we can kill it."

"Damn it, Nick, will you STOP with the Predator, Alien, Aliens, and all the other stupid movie quotes."

"Cass, love, people who annoy people; they are the luckiest people in the world. Howie Mandel said that. Words to live by."

Ragnar held up an *I Got This* palm, causing Cass to hold her response. "Those people who think they know everything are a great annoyance to those of us who do. Isaac Asimov."

Nick was chuckling, hardly getting the words out. "Would you look at that! Ragnar made a joke."

Cass felt the need to defend her husband. "Nick, Ragnar has a sense of humor."

"Of course, he does. It just never appears."

Bonnie conceded. "Some people can't believe in themselves until someone else believes in them first."

Everyone turned to Bonnie, surprised and amused. Cass recognized the reference. "Sean Maguire in Good Will Hunting. Nick, I think she understands."

Nick agrees. "Yes, Cass, I think she does."

Cass continues mentoring. "Bonnie, there are planets full of people who believe in your father. Billions of people believe in The Redeemer. But that means nothing to the simple truth of how we have survived the many missions.

"What did Nick say once ... oh yeah. 'That's what I like about our Texas Cowboy. There's never any bullshit. We are running forward, eyes closed, going to get a whole lot of dead but, what the hell, we will figure it out.'

"The simple truth Bonnie, is we believe in each other."

Bonnie is smiling, understanding, looking from person to person, receiving smiles in return. When she ends with Cass, Ragnar returns to form. "Landry, status, please."

"Lucinda is maintaining course and velocity. She will be joined in five hours by Corb and Janish. The math says we will drop into standard space two lightyears from Megves Major. Below the elliptical plane, approximately point-five lightyears off-center.

"Of course, we are estimating where Megves Major is in its solar orbit. Recommend stealth mode on emergence."

Ragnar does not miss a beat. "Confirmed, stealth mode on emergence. We are going to rotate shifts early. We want the first shift at emergence. Landry, request second shift report to the bridge."

Dugr, Bridge

Time to emergence: 00:00:30

The light emanating from the riser symbols is fading. The second shift did not leave the bridge after their short duty assignment. The monitors change from the blue-green hue of the trilateral domain to a starfield.

Lucinda is on-point. "Landry report."

"We are two-point-two lightyears from the Megves star. Megves Major is ninety-degrees relative to our current position. I can adjust our position."

"No, stand firm. I presume we are a hole in space?"

"Confirmed. Stealth mode active, no emissions."

"Initiate passive scans."

The first shift crew's tension is real. Years of emerging from hyper-tunnels into an ambush left a black mark on their collective psyche. The new crew notices the older crew's tightness.

"Confirmed. Passive scans."

Red dots begin appearing on the monitors.

"Landry?"

"Captain, those are Megvesnaith attack fighters, transport vessels, and carriers."

"That's just f'n great. How many?"

"Five complete carrier groups."

"Carriers?"

"Yes, Ragnar, there are five carriers. The attack fighters and transports have formed a defensive perimeter on their assigned carrier."

"Landry, how many?"

"Captain?"

"How many of everything?"

"Five carriers. Fifteen transport vessels. Three-hundred and twenty-five attack fighters. Of course, using passive scans, those are only the ships we can see. There are likely additional fighters on the carriers."

"Captain, this is not a raiding party."

"No, Corey, it is not."

"Something very big is going to happen here."

"Damn it, Nick. A Predator quote again? Really? Enough with the movie! ... At least get some new quotes."

"But captain, they are going to squeeze our friends, and we can't let that happen."

No one giggled at Nick's comment. Lucinda realizes Corey and Nick have figured it out. She waits, glaring at Nick. Nick's formal response is a surprise to the new crew. "Captain, it is an invasion force."

"I agree. But which planet? Earth?"

"Planets."

"What, Corb?"

"Planets. Plural. The ships headed to Sol are a probe or a diversion. They probably wanted me to stay and defend Sol. They sent the probe, not expecting me to leave Sol. They are planning on invading five or six planets. Landry, can we tap their communications?"

"Yes, Corb, but there is a problem. They are running silent."

"Oh shit."

Corb agrees with the captain. "Yes, Lucinda, oh shit."

Bonnie does not understand the concern. "What?"

Lucinda educates Bonnie. "It means they are about to depart. Landry, where is the hyper-tunnel entrance?"

A blue diamond appears on the monitors.

"Captain, they are mustering for departure."

"Correct, Corey. Landry, which sentient planet is closest?"

A green diamond appears on the monitors. Three hyper-tunnel segments appear.

"The Nanov System. Three billion sentients."

"Landry discontinue scans. Make us a dark hole. No one knows we are here. Everyone, stand down for three hours. Beth, you have the con. Do nothing. Sit here and wait."

The tension and tone in Lucinda's voice are striking.

"Does everyone understand? Do nothing!"

In unison, "Yes, Captain."

"Landry, I want you to generate scenarios. I want to know where they are going and what they plan to do when they get there. All-hands to meet in the galley in three hours. Dismissed."

Dugr, Galley

"Landry, confirm for me the premise."

"Cass, the most likely scenario is Megves Major is no longer capable of supporting the Megvesnaith people. They have developed a colonization strategy. The scenarios from the analysis indicate these six systems are the targets."

"Six? There are five carrier groups."

"Correct. Do not forget about the ships on the way to Sol. They are likely a carrier group also. Because Sol is the furthest location, the carrier groups are departing on a schedule that will put them on their respective targets simultaneously."

"Isn't this the dog's dinner?"

Landry responds to the British slang. "Yes, Nick, this is a mess. They appear to have a well-coordinated invasion effort underway. Captain, shall I display and present the most likely scenario?"

"Yes, Landry."

The monitors change into the image for the Orion Spur. Six color-coded flight paths, using the hyper-tunnel network, appear.

"As you can see, Sol, on the green hyper-tunnel path, is the furthest from the Megves system. The next carrier will enter the hyper-tunnel in approximately three hours. Followed by the remaining carrier groups, in order, on the schedule you see posted.

"The six carrier groups will arrive at their respective targets in approximately four weeks."

"Four weeks!?!"

"Yes, Janish, four weeks. The scenarios indicate the covert operations to determine the nature and timing of the Megvesnaith group headed to Sol were inaccurate."

Corey oozes sarcasm. "Of course, it was inaccurate."

Landry's avatar stopped and focused on the interrupter. Corey was surprised to feel chastised by the AI's holographic projection.

"Apologies, I will remain silent. Landry, please continue."

"The analysis indicates the invasion forces will be successful. Captain, Earth is in danger."

"Thank you, Landry. Discussion."

Lucinda pointed to Cass to begin the debate.

"Why now? What changed?

"Good question. Landry?"

"Unknown."

"Are you telling me you have nothing?"

"Nothing until we go active with our scans. Everything at this point is speculation."

"Got it. NT?"

"One: Head to the nearest communications relay and blast the message. Let people know what is happening. Two: Straight line to Sol. Defend earth. Blow these bastards apart as they emerge."

"Got it. Warn everyone. Kickass. Take names. Let everyone fight their own battle. Not sure I agree, but okay. Nick?"

"It's only after we've lost everything that we're free to do anything."

"I know that one ... wait ... Fight Club?"

"Right-O!"

"You are saying something bad happened to force the Megvesnaith into this?"

"Correct."

"Interesting. Janish?"

"I have no comment other than we need to get home and defend Earth."

"Cass?"

"Same as Janish, get home and defend Earth."

"Ragnar?"

"We need to know more, a lot more. Why now? What changed? Is there something or someone behind this? I like NT's idea, but we gather data first. We need to know more."

"Agreed."

Turning her seat to face the standing crew from the second shift, each shook their head in the negative, indicating they have nothing to add.

"Beth, I am not going to let you remain silent. Do you want to be a captain? Tell me what a captain would do."

"Lucinda, I have an opinion, but I want to hear from Corb and Bonnie first."

"That might be the smartest thing you have ever said."

Lucinda turned to Bonnie with a look of inquisition.

"Augment Ragnar's plan. Let's go scan Megves Major up close. Gather data, then make a decision."

"Interesting. You think there is something wrong with Megves Major?"

"I do."

"Why?"

"There are no points. No connections anywhere close that are not in the direction of the carrier groups."

Realizing the significance of Bonnie's summation, Lucinda turned to Corb.

"She is correct. There are no connections in this system that are not on one of those ships."

"We need to be fresh. Getting here was a real tax. Everyone takes a break. Stand down for an hour. Landry, monitor everything. You know the drill. Get us up here if anything happens."

"Confirmed. We are a hole in space."

Dugr, Bonnie's Cabin

Corey insisted on a meeting with Bonnie. His whining has not decreased.

"What if they find out?"

"You don't think they already know?"

"How could they?"

"Come on, Corey, these people have been fighting for Earth since before you and I were born. They did not survive by being stupid."

"But ..."

"No buts ... You need to stop alienating Beth. She is an excellent officer and will be a captain one day.

"No, you are not going to sleep here. This is not Geneva and the TCCA. That was then, and this is now. It is a different time, and I am a different person."

Bonnie's vest and undershirt expose her arms. Corey is staring at the colored scars. "What happened to you?"

"Happened? Nothing? I completed the Plentari Military Academy training."

"Yes, I know that, but what happened? You used to talk all the time. Now ... Now you only talk when someone asks you a question. What happened?"

"Corey, I learned what is important and what is meaningless. We are overwhelmed with the meaningless. This mission is important. What we had ... I am sorry, what we had is not important."

"It was important then."

"Yes, that is how it felt to two people too

young to know the difference. It was a fling, nothing more. I am no longer that person. Do you think we should go to Megves Major?"

Corey realizes she is changing the subject. He attempts to move closer. Bonnie softly raises her hand. An unseen force is gently pushing him back.

"Bonnie, why?"

"You know why. Do you think we should go to Megves Major?"

"Yes. Find out what happened, if anything, then head to Sol. We need to warn people. We need to develop a plan to defend Earth."

"I agree, but we also need a plan to help the other systems under attack."

"Why? Our duty is to Sol and Earth."

"Why should we help others? Because they are people, and they have helped Earth. We need a better plan."

Corey realizes the discussion is pointless. Whatever he and Bonnie had once is gone. Unable to speak, suddenly feeling very lonely on a ship full of people, he turns to leave. Bonnie watches the hatch close behind Corey, thinking.

He is a disappointment.
One time ...
I was naïve.
Now, I understand.
I thought he was mentally stronger.

Like so many, he is weak.
Beth is strong.
She can lead.
Maybe JJ.
I need to know more about JJ.
I will challenge him to a Contest.
Yes, a Contest.
Maybe Beth is the key.
Not a Contest, JJ will not agree to combat
with a Plentari Warrior.
He will know.
JJ knows the legends.
He knows the legend of Aalborinn.
Under the stars, she will not look away.
Maybe JJ.

Part Two

Some destinies are inevitable.

Dugr, Galley

"Lucinda, I have an idea."

"Let's hear it, Corb."

"Landry has corrected his estimates for the Megvesnaith attacks. The soonest the ships headed to Sol will arrive at about two-and-one-half months, based on the new information. About seventy-five days.

"Using the new slipstream rotation technique, we can reach Sol in under ten days from here. If the assumption of a simultaneous attack profile is correct, the next carrier group will depart in less than one hour. The planet K'an is their likely target. Landry?"

Corb pointed to the monitors and the now-familiar projections of the Megvesnaith attack vectors.

"Stringing back along the projected attack trajectories, these planets are the most probable targets."

"Plentari?"

"Yes, JJ, Plentari. Lucinda, I propose if the next carrier group departs on the projected timeline, we act. We go hot. We force their hand."

"Okay, tell me more."

The crew listened to Corb describe his plan. They critiqued, altered, adjusted, and agreed to the reconnaissance plan.

Dugr, **Bridge**

The entire crew was on the bridge to support the reconnaissance plan.

"Captain?"

"Yes, Landry?'

"The carrier group we designated as Beta is making for the hyper-tunnel emergence point."

"Right on schedule. Nick, put us on that planet."

"Course plotted."

"Landry?"

"Nick's jump calculations are correct."

"We are going hot, people. These bastards are going to know we are here in about thirty seconds.

"Be sharp. Nick, let's go."

The *Dugr* responded to Nick's pressing the correct series of icons. Using its internal star-portal mechanism, the big ship jumped in-system, precisely as planned, one-hundred thousand kilometers above the Megves Prime equatorial plane.

"Nick?"

"We hit the target. Five-by-five."

"Ragnar?"

"No threats. No ships. Nothing. Five-by-five."

"Odd. Landry?"

"Captain, the planet is uninhabited. The planet is capable of supporting life thirty-three degrees above and twenty-two degrees below the equatorial plane. The poles are too cold for biological life to thrive."

"What do you mean, uninhabited."

"Captain, the scanners are not able to identify any life on the planet."

"None?"

"Correct, no biological life. There may be artificial life, but that is also unlikely. There are no power emissions. The satellite network is non-existent."

"Non-existent? Explain."

"No satellites are orbiting Megves Major."

Lucinda's tense voice continued. "Either

something terrible happened here, or we walked into a trap. Give me the long-range images."

The bridge's monitors changed from a long-range shot of the planet to several close-up views of Megves Prime.

Megves Major is a wasteland.

The images are of cities comprised of pyramids. Tens of thousands of pyramids. Small dwellings and large, complex metropolitan structures.

"Enhance."

The monitors zoom to three of the large city complexes. Decay is evident in the run-down buildings and crumbling infrastructure. All of the natural areas are empty wastelands.

"This did not happen overnight. Something bad happened. Landry, using the size of the buildings and the number of city complexes, estimate the population. Extrapolate, are the six carrier groups capable of holding the Megvesnaith population?"

"Stand by ...

"Estimates put the Megvesnaith population between five-hundred million and one-point-five billion. The carrier groups have a total estimated capacity to support one-hundred and eighty thousand."

Janish breaks the silence. "Where did they go?"

The images shift, zoom, pan, then focus on

several large structures.

"Landry?"

"Captain, those are the answer to Janish's question."

"Explain."

"What you are seeing are ash mounds from pyres."

"Biomass. That is what you do with billions of corpses. Pyres. Bloody 'ell, they are kilometers across."

"Nick, they are just under seven kilometers wide by six kilometers tall. Captain, the closest carrier group, has sortied two squadrons to our location. They will arrive in forty-seven minutes."

"Nick, get us out of here."

The *Dugr*'s jump put the ship further from the carrier groups.

"We are dark."

"Thank you, Nick."

Lucinda scanned the bridge. No one chose to speak or offer an opinion. Waiting, Lucinda focused on Bonnie.

"They had to leave ... They cannot come home. There is no home to come back to ..."

"Do you have any idea why?"

"No."

"Landry, did you do your magic while we were on station? Did you gather any electronic intel?"

"No, Captain. There are no electronic

emissions in this system. Their carriers are completely silent, or we do not know how to access their communication technologies."

Lucinda was about to issue orders when Corey stepped over her, in full-whine mode.

"That's fucking great. We gave away our advantage, and all we know now that we did not know before is the planet is dead. We don't know why it is dead. We think we know where the carrier groups are headed, but we can't stop them.

"Captain, do all your missions run this well?"

Disgusted at the outburst, Bonnie is not above doling out corporal punishment. Corey grabs his throat before falling to the deck, unconscious. The fall breaks his nose.

"Bonnie!"

"Sorry, Captain. He was out of line."

"Yes, he was out of line, but it is not your place to issue punishment. Punishment, when required, is the Captain's responsibility."

"Yes, I know, I am sorry. Captain, do you know Corey was put here by the TC3 Security Council?"

"I am aware. The TC3 Security Council is trying to gather information to wrest control of the TC3 from the civilian leadership. We are not going to let that happen. Now, however, you are confined to your quarters. I will review the regulations for the appropriate punishment.

"NT, JJ, pick him up, get him fixed up, and

put him in his cabin."

Bonnie stepped over the prone Corey on her way to her cabin with a sidelong glance of disdain. NT and JJ roughly drag the unconscious crewman to the medical bay. When the bridge hatch closes, Corb speaks for the first time.

"Lucinda, she will learn, remember this is her first mission. She did not know she was going to be on a mission six weeks ago."

"Understood, but she hurt him for mouthing off. Is that her personality, or is it the Plentari training?"

"Yes, she did hurt him. Let's ask JJ what he knows about the Plentari warrior training. Right now, we need to figure out what we are going to do about the invasion forces."

"Agreed. Do you think your backup plan is in motion?"

"I do, but now I think it might not be enough."

Dugr, Bridge

After standing down for several hours, Lucinda has ordered the entire crew back to the bridge.

"Where are we?"

"Two lightyears above the elliptical plane and another half a lightyear further from the remaining carriers."

"Thanks, Nick. Opinions?"

Shocking to Lucinda, everyone remained silent.

"Okay, theorize?"

Everyone looked at their captain with fear and confusion.

"Well, damn. Landry, run an analysis. What happened here?"

"Captain, I anticipated the request. The asked for analysis is complete."

"Well?"

"Captain, the highest probability is the Megvesnaith have outgrown Megves Major. They are planning to conquer and occupy six systems. They are creating a network of homeworlds from which they can plunder the surrounding star systems."

"Will they be successful?"

"Yes, but several systems will resist the colonization for several years."

Lucinda understood the implications. She turned to Corb. "What does The Redeemer have to say about this little cluster?"

Winking at Lucinda, Corb turns to Bonnie and asks a question. "Bonnie, have you seen this in your Second Sight?"

"Yes."

"Would you care to elaborate?"

"No."

Lucinda was not willing to take no for an answer. "I like your resolve, but that is not how it works out here. You are here, on the bridge, because confinement to your cabin reduces our team's effectiveness. Your punishment will be determined later. Now, if you have information that may help our situation, you need to share it."

"You won't like it."

Nick snickered and chirped. "Little Bit, there isn't a whole lot we do like about being out in the middle of nowhere with no backup. That is kind of how it goes for this merry band of miscreants.

"The only rule we follow is: Don't get dead.

"So, go ahead, bad news does not get better with time. Besides, it can't be any worse than what we have faced in the past."

Looking from person to person, Bonnie received nods of affirmation.

"We can't save them all. At least one, maybe two systems will fall to the Megvesnaith."

"You have seen this in your Second Sight?"

"Yes, Cass. Father, do you remember?"

"Yes, I remember."

In silence, everyone waited for Corb to elaborate.

"Bonnie asked me about the Megvesnaith when she was about eleven. She had known this day was coming since before we returned from the Muh'xan expedition."

"See, right there! A fookin' decade and it is

still the same with you. Corb, when were you going to mention these IMPORTANT LITTLE DETAILS?"

Corb does not rise to Nick's frustration. His response is calm and even. "Nick, would it have made any difference? We'd still be right here, right now. If I had told you what we thought might happen, would anything be different?"

"We might feel like a team and not the folks whose job it is to pull your arse from the fire."

"Granted. If I happen upon an eleven-year-old girl telling me a story about the boogie man, I will let you know ASAP."

Having said his piece, Nick winked at Corb's remark and remained silent. Corb's grin let everyone know he does not mind verbal challenges.

"We need a plan. Of course, Earth and Plentari are the priority. We warn the others, but do we let them fall? Which system will fall first, who will hold out the longest? Earth and Plentari are highly vulnerable. K'an ... My guess is K'an has their defenses planned. Who knows what new deal those bastards cut.

"Landry, using the new rotation in the trilateral slipstream, estimate the time to transit from Plentari to Earth."

"I have refined the quantum calculations. Using the rotation model, We were traveling faster than we understood. From Plentari to Earth, using the new rotation is three-point-nine days."

"Wow. Okay. Estimate how long from here to Plentari?"

"Four-point-five days."

"There's our answer."

Lucinda was nodding, looking around. "Nick, plot a course to Plentari. First shift stand-down. JJ, come with us."

JJ and the first shift depart the bridge. Corey, bandaged nose muffling his voice, is unable to remain quiet. "Why are we going to Plentari? Earth is the priority."

Beth's tone is even. "We are going to Plentari because that is what the captain said we are going to do. What is wrong with you? Did you learn anything at the academy?"

"I learned to ask questions, and I do not like the answers I am getting or not getting."

Beth intercedes. "Bonnie, what do you know?"

"I know people are going to die. Lots of people are going to die, and there is nothing we can do about it."

Corey continues his whine. "I thought the captain confined you to your quarters for assaulting me?"

"She did. You heard her. She rescinded the order. We need all hands to figure this out. Put that in your report. Put it all in your report, including your whining. Make sure you get it all and add the videos."

"Videos?"

"Yes, moron, videos. Landry?"

"All crew activities, not specific to their private quarters, are recorded."

Corey's already pale face turned ashen.

"I see you understand the implications. Openly challenging the captain does not look good. Some might say I put down the seed of a mutiny."

Afraid, Corey turns to his console, killing the conversation.

Beth smiled with a wink for Bonnie.

Dugr, Galley

"JJ, please sit. We have some questions for you."

Taking a seat at the far end of the table, JJ understands Lucinda's request is an order. The entire first shift crew is seated at the other end of the table. Lucinda opens the discussion.

"The Plentari Military Training Academy, what can you tell us about it?"

"The Academy? It is for training Plentari warriors. It produces elite warriors."

"Yes, thank you. We understand its role and have read about the severity of its training requirements. What we want to understand is what kind of warriors does it produce."

Realizing there is an undercurrent of worry, JJ sits up and responds.

"You are asking me if the training changes people. The answer to that question is yes. But, Redeemer, you knew that was a possibility. No one who survives the academy training is the same after the instruction."

"Survives?"

"Yes, the training is very demanding. Many of the trainees do not survive."

"When you say they are not the same after training, how are they not the same?"

"Plentari warriors are fierce. They have an unbending will to serve. The warriors trained at the academy are the most revered and the most feared."

Lucinda looks to Corb, who continues the questioning.

"Fierce is a very human word. Are you sure that is the correct word?"

"Fierce: Possessing an intense or ferocious aggressiveness. Yes, Redeemer, fierce is the correct word."

"Call me, Corb. JJ, do you think Bonnie is fierce?"

"Redeemer, the rumors are many. Bonnie is known to be the fiercest warrior for which the academy has conferred the stripes."

Cass interrupted. "Stripes?"

"Yes, on her left arm, there are markings."

Corb resumed the questioning. "I understand. Your mother had the marks. You said rumors. Tell me about the rumors."

"It is said, Redeemer, your daughter received the request for the Contest every cycle."

"Wait, let me understand. Bonnie was challenged to battle every day. She fought every day?"

"That is correct, Redeemer, according to the rumors."

"Is this common? To fight every day?"

"I do not know. No males are permitted to know academy training."

"Speculate."

"Redeemer, it is known: Aalborinn, Daughter of the Redeemer, First Daughter of the Plentari is undefeated in battle.

"The Madame Negotiator herself put the marks on Aalborinn's arm."

"I understand. Anything else?"

"Redeemer, there is no Plentari alive who can defeat Aalborinn in combat."

Death to All, Bridge

"Captain, Did the squadrons make their departure times?"

"Yes, Commodore, all squadrons departed on schedule."

"Is there any reason we are sitting here like a Chestnut Pademelon's turd stinking up the garden?"

"Commodore, it is my place to advise you. My advice to you is the same as it was when we received the request."

"Yes, Captain, your weak heart does not want to leave our home undefended. Open the fleet-wide intercom."

The captain complies.

"Attention, this is Commodore Jexond. We are about to depart for the mission. We will complete our mission or die bravely in the service of those who gave us much.

"I remind you all. We control this system because of our loyalty.

"I remind you all. Because of our loyalty, we enjoy life twice as long as was planned."

"I remind you all, your existence is to serve. Serve and die when necessary.

"We depart for the mission, do not fear for your homeworld. I have taken precautions. For those whose luck favors a long life, you will return to your home, as it is today.

"Commodore Jexond, out."

He turned to his executive officer, who is visibly nervous. "Yes, XO, I am aware of your plans. Commander, open the video link."

The bridge monitors flip to an image of Ajawlil storm troopers bursting into a conference room. The soldiers kill everyone. Turning to the camera, the masked squad leader speaks. "Commodore Jexond, the rebellion has been put down. We await news of your glorious victory."

If Ajawlil clones possessed sweat glands, the XO would be soaked.

"Commander, execute the XO, and assume his role and rank."

The commander does not flinch. He shoots the captain in the face. Two orderlies rush in to drag away the body. Two additional orderlies begin cleaning laser charred blood and brains from the bulkhead. The commander, who is now the captain and XO, turns to the navigation station.

"Make for the entrance. We have a mission to complete."

Dugr, Galley

Lucinda speaks between bites of a toasted muffin with jam.

"Before we cut the second shift loose, any new ideas?"

Beth speaks up. "Captain, Corey had an idea."

Surprised by the vote of confidence, the crew turn to Corey, who spoke through his bandaged nose.

"It comes down to a simple equation. Who do we help? First, we get back to the communication network and warn the sentient planets. We inform all of them. Give everyone our analysis. We encrypt a second message for the leadership of the six systems we expect to be targeted by the Megvesnaith.

"A warning is the first step.

"The second step is above my paygrade. Who do we help, and who do we let fall?"

Corb listens to a long debate of morals, ethics, and politics. He notices Bonnie is ignoring the conversation, but she occasionally looks up and catches Corb's eye. After a long circular debate, he closes the discussion. "Landry, can we hurt one of those carriers?"

"Yes, but the *Dugr* will be damaged in the attack. Each carrier's attack fighters are in a defensive profile."

"Lucinda?"

"Okay, Corb. Landry, run some simulations. I want to know if we can survive taking out one of those carriers before we head out."

"Confirmed."

Landry's avatar has not dissipated. The projected image is watching NT, waiting for a reaction. NT says nothing until everyone focuses on him. When he has everyone's attention, he looks to Corb with his response. "Sophie's choice."

Corb's grin tells the experienced crew he has a plan. His two words resonate with his friends. "It is not Sophie's choice. It is the Kobayashi Maru."

Janish erupted using Nick's sarcastic accent. "Bloody well right, change the rules, but don't tell anyone."

***Dugr*, Bridge**

"Beth, I thought I told the second shift to stand down."

"You did. We want to know the plan."

"Fair enough. Landry?"

"Captain, I was able to complete one thousand and six...

"I don't need the background. What did you find?"

"There is a ninety-four percent probability of the *Dugr* receiving significant damage during an attack on a Megvesnaith carrier. A three percent chance we will not survive the encounter."

Lucinda ignored the not survive part of the report. "Got it. We get hurt. Two questions. One, how bad do we get hurt? Two, can we destroy or take a carrier out of the mix?"

"Question one. The Megvesnaith fighters will be behind us when we attack. Consequently, we are likely to lose one or both of the engines.

"It will require a stop at a maintenance depot to repair the damage."

"Will we still be able to fly?"

"Yes. Assuming no engines, we can use maneuvering thrusters to create momentum. We will use the generated momentum for the Triad to initiate the trilateral slipstream."

"Got it. Question two? Can we take a carrier

offline?"

"Yes. However, the probability is the damaged carrier's attack fighters will be ordered to augment the other carriers."

"Understood. Are the attack fighters interstellar capable?"

"No. The attack fighters require a carrier for interstellar transport."

"Rerun the simulations. This time, wait until three of the remaining carriers have departed."

"Understood. Stand by."

Lucinda turned in the direction of Cass, who was clearing her throat. "Lucinda, you can't be serious. How long do you plan to wait? Is the damage we will take worth the risk to Earth?"

"Cass, your concern is noted. They gave me the big girl panties for exactly these decisions."

Ragnar put on his executive officer hat. "Understood, Captain. However, can we get the repairs completed and arrive at Sol in time to defend Earth?"

"Landry modify the parameters. Factor in repairs at Kripkeni Station and transit to Sol."

"Confirmed, repair time, and transit to Sol."

Ragnar takes an unusually familiar tone with his follow-on concern. "Lucinda, I know you want to take out a carrier. Everyone wants to take out a carrier group, but defending Sol is the priority."

"Cass, what have you done to our Ragnar? He's a nice guy. Ragnar, I want all options before

I make a decision."

"Understood."

Turning with a grim expression, Lucinda continues. "Beth, speak."

"Captain, damaging the *Dugr*, putting the ship at risk, before we warn the other worlds, before we have a plan we trust, is not a good decision."

Lucinda raises an eyebrow at the direct response. Beth stood her ground. "You asked."

"Yes, I did. Here is the new plan. Landry, how far can we stand-off from the first carrier and put rail guns in its side? Assuming it has docked its attack fighters, and it is more than one minute from entering the hyper-tunnel."

Frowns and grimaces turned to smiles of realization.

"Three to thirty thousand meters. Assuming a targeting profile of the *Dugr* standing off directly abeam of the carrier. Positioned between two o'clock and five o'clock, or ten o'clock and seven o'clock."

Nodding affirmatively at the new information, Lucinda issued the order. "We stand-off at ten thousand meters. Create a flight profile. Either side, I don't care. Nick, check his work. Ragnar plot a firing solution.

"We are going to kill carrier Charlie just before it enters the hyper-tunnel.

"Landry, when we jump into ten-thousand

meters, how long before the carrier Delta's fighters can reach us?"

"Estimate, four minutes, twenty seconds."

"Ragnar, you have three minutes. I want carrier Charlie dead in three minutes. Nick, start at the top and slide down, give Ragnar the profile arc.

"Questions?

"None?

"Landry, monitor carrier Charlie closely. I want to be ready before it moves."

"Confirmed, it has recalled its fighters. I estimate it will reach the entry point in fifty-six minutes."

Bonnie catches Lucinda's eye.

"It is a good plan. We kill the carrier, leave the debris. It will slow down the remaining carriers. That leaves five systems at risk. What is your plan after we send the communications? Once the information is out there, everyone who feels vulnerable will be begging for help. They will need more than a warning. They will need assurance."

Lucinda nodded, acknowledging she understood Bonnie's question before turning to Corb. "We'll take out the carrier then B-line for Plentari."

Bonnie does not accept the response. "What about Earth?"

Corb winks. "Leave Sol to me."

Everyone realizes the discussion has ended.

The crew quietly and efficiently prepare to attack the Megevesnaith carrier designated Charlie.

"Nick?"

Lucinda's chirp surprised everyone and masked an order. Nick begins his mission report after pressing a few icons. His flight profile appears on the monitors.

"Lucinda, we are going to use our badass emergency jump feature to position the *Dugr* on the green diamond. It will put us at two o'clock, ten-K meters off the invasion carrier's starboard beam. We will drop on the z-axis keeping our forward shields a-beam of the invasion ship.

"Assuming we don't take fire from the carrier, they do not appear to be outfitted with heavy guns. We should be in and out in under three minutes. Ragnar?"

"We will charge the railguns before we jump on target. I will need six seconds to confirm targeting before the first volley. To maintain as much fire as possible, we will alternate the rail guns, port followed by starboard.

"Alternating the recharging and loading, we can put seventeen volleys on target in three minutes."

"Thank you, gentlemen.

"Questions?

"Great. Everyone strap in. Beth duplicate my console using Janish's science station. JJ observe

Ragnar's console from NT's station."

"Captain, the carrier Charlie is moving toward the hyper-tunnel entrance. ETA to the hyper-tunnel entrance horizon, eighty-three seconds."

"Thank you, Landry. If there are no objections? Nick, let's kill a carrier."

The big ship responded to Nick's fingers. Dropping the stealth mode, jumping to the designated point, the *Dugr* arrived just as the carrier came into range.

"Nick?"

"We missed high by seven-hundred meters. Otherwise, we are on the mark."

"Ragnar?"

"Fire control adjusted. Firing in twelve…

"Ten…"

JJ barks. "She's rolling."

"Got it. Five, four, three, two, firing."

The shrieking of three, three-ton heavy-metal rail-gun bolts surprised the new crew.

"Thirty-two seconds to impact."

The crew heard the second volley of heavy-metal rail-gun bolts scream through the *Dugr's* superstructure.

The first volley tore into the carrier just above the starboard chine. Before the second volley exploded into the Megvesnaith carrier, the third rail gun volley screamed away from the *Dugr*.

"Captain, fighters have been scrambled from

carrier Delta."

"Thank you, Landry. Ragnar?"

"None of the rail gun bolts have exited the carrier or created significant damage. The carrier's mass is absorbing the artillery. Recommend targeting their engines."

"Agreed. Landry, target their engines."

Ragnar waited two seconds for the new fire control parameters to appear on his console. He did a quick check before reporting.

"New fire control, confirmed. JJ?"

"Fire control confirmed."

Ragnar paused, then resumed in his dry, bright tone. "Firing in three, two, firing."

Everyone stopped cringing at the harsh sound of death issued by the *Dugr's* rail guns.

"Impact in four, three, two...

"Direct hit. I got explosions. They are venting atmo.

"Impact in three, two...

"Damn. Two of the bolts bounced off the hull due to the carrier's roll. Compensating."

"Wait! Look. What is that?"

Cass's bark yanked everyone's attention toward the monitors. The images of the carrier were astonishing. A large reddish-black form was oozing from the midship gashes created by the first rail-gun volleys.

"Landry?"

"Captain, it is an unknown substance."

"Ragnar, keep the rail guns firing at the engines. Put the plasma cannons on that blob. Landry?"

"Plasma cannon fire control loaded."

"Ragnar?"

"Firing."

The crew watched the lasers intersect the blob. Where they hit the blob, massive holes emerged, but the lasers continued into the void of space.

"We know it is not solid. What, the hell, is it?"

"Captain, it is blood."

"Say that again, Landry."

"Confirmed, it is blood."

"How much? Never mind that now. What is going on?"

Ragnar continues to fire the rail guns at the carrier's aft fuselage while Lucinda responds to Landry's raised hand.

"Captain, I recommend targeting the carrier's reactors. Rupture their antimatter containment field. It will destroy the ship and everything it is expelling."

"Agreed, but we are too close for the shields to absorb an antimatter explosion. Nick?"

"I can get us out of here."

"Are you sure? This is a one-shot deal."

"Lucinda, I got this."

"Good. Landry load the fire control. Ragnar

fire when ready."

NT jumped ahead of Landry's reporting. "The first attack fighter will be in range in twenty-nine seconds."

Ragnar was unmoved by the warning. "Roger that, fighters in twenty-nine seconds. JJ, you own the short-range defensive lasers."

"Understood."

Lucinda's voice was calm. "Ragnar?"

"Firing."

Simultaneously, both rail guns screamed, and the four forward plasma cannons erupted. The weapons focused on a single point, just forward of the carrier's main engine nacelles. The plasma lasers ignored the carrier's weak composite shielding and bored a hole into the carrier.

The rail gun bolts followed the plasma cannons. Three of the six bolts found the invader's hull. The other three found the hole created by the plasma lasers.

"NICK!"

The *Dugr* disappeared and reappeared two lightyears from the hyper-tunnel entrance. At two lightyears, the carrier's antimatter confinement rupture's bright flash caused the monitors to kick-in their light filters.

"Good flying Nick. Landry?"

"The carrier we designated Charlie was destroyed. I am picking up communications between the other carriers. Their fleet Commander is aboard the invasion ship that we assigned the designation Golf.

"The explosion disabled carrier Delta. Seven hundred and twelve Delta carrier's fighters were destroyed, or their pilots were killed in the blast. Carrier Echo is maneuvering to offload carrier Delta's cargo. Carrier Fox-Trot is moving to clear the area in front of the hyper-tunnel entrance.

"They have new orders. All invasion forces will make for their targets as quickly as possible."

"Landry, can you access their computers?"

"Yes, Cass."

"What are they carrying?"

"They are carrying blood."

"Blood? Is it their food source?"

"Yes, Cass, but it is also their primary weapon."

"Weapon?"

"Yes, weapon."

Lucinda spoke with urgency. "Hold those thoughts. Corb, Janish, let's blow this pop stand."

The Triad turned their chairs inward at the corners of the triangular riser. Nick pressed the icon sequence that got the big ship moving. The crew felt the big engines and grabbed their black-out goggles.

"One second, Lucinda, I need to check on something." Using his nanobots, Corb confirms his backup plan is in motion.

"Landry?"

"Yes, Corb?"

"Use the micro-wormhole communication device. Send the messages alpha-one through alpha-nine."

"Confirming, initiate the micro-wormhole connection and transmit messages alpha-one through alpha-nine."

"Confirmed."

"The message transit will require at least seventeen hours."

"Understood, send them anyway. I don't need a reply. The information is too important to wait until we can find a comms relay."

"Understood. Establishing a link now."

"I sent update messages. Go ahead, Lucinda."

"Nick?"

"Captain, point six *c* in twenty-four seconds."

The light from the riser symbols was intense. The Triad's collective adrenalin pushed the *Dugr* into the FTL conduit quicker than any previous entry. Lucinda and Janish turned away, letting Corb control the wave. Lucinda was issuing the orders on her way off the bridge.

"Second shift, you have the con. Shift change in ten hours. Bonnie, I want you to report with the first shift."

As the crew departed the bridge, Corb is controlling the trilateral slipstream. Bonnie felt her father's connection reach out, checking on her mental state.

He wants me to know he is watching.
He knows something.
Something important.
He knows I have to do something.
I need to speak to JJ.
JJ will know.

Death to All, Bridge

The Death to All is transiting from the prior emergence point to the next entry point between hyper-tunnels. The transit time between hyper-tunnels is a respite for the crew and time to make repairs.

"Commodore, we have received a secure message."

"I will take it in my ready room."

The massive commodore, resplendent in his gaudy purple and gold uniform, waddles off the bridge to his ready room. As he enters his sanctuary, the daybed-like reclining chaise lowers, allowing his fat mass to lounge. The day bed recliner rises. A monitor drops from the ceiling and swings into place.

The commodore's sausage-like fingers press the correct icons to read the secure message.

Shocked at what he is reading, he rolls himself off the recliner, pushes up to his full height, knocking the monitor askew.

Storming onto the bridge, he is issuing orders before he reclines in the command chair.

"Navigation, how long before arrival?"

"Commodore, three transits are remaining. We will arrive in-system in twenty-seven cycles."

"That is too long. I want you to enter the next hyper-tunnel at point five-five *c*."

"But, Commodore, we do not know if the stress of entry at that speed will be damaging to the hull."

"I am well aware of the risks. If you question my orders again, I will have you replaced. Captain, enter every hyper-tunnel at point five-five *c*. Do you understand?"

The captain looks to the lieutenant sitting at the navigation station and receives a confirmation nod before responding.

"Point five-five *c*. Confirmed. May I inquire, what changed?"

"We must engage the enemy when they emerge from the hyper-tunnel. They cannot be permitted to travel in-system."

Plentari, Main Meeting Hall

"Madame Negotiator, we cannot let the attackers into our system. I recommend we position our forces to intercept the Megvesnaith in the barren quadrant designated Zeon-One-Alpha-Eighty-One."

"Admiral, that is a worthy suggestion. What information do you have to confirm the Megvesnaith will transit via the barren quadrant?"

"Madame Negotiator, the information we received indicates the attack routes."

"You are taking liberty with the information. The message is clear. The analysis is a probability. We cannot be completely confident they will attack from the direction indicated."

"Madame Negotiator, we cannot let the attackers into our system."

"Admiral, if you are wrong, if they come from another direction, we will have dispersed our forces and will be unable to repel the attackers.

"The humans have a saying. They call it an adage. The Plentari can learn from human maxims.

"Admiral, we will make our stand at the emergence point. Sixty percent of our forces at the projected emergence point. Thirty percent halfway to the second emergence point. The last ten percent remain in orbit to augment the planetary defenses.

"Admiral, prepare your troops for the final sacrifice."

"Madame Negotiator, the final sacrifice will

not be required. We have overwhelming numbers. The carriers will not be able to launch their fleet before we are victorious."

Stepping off her dais, the Madame Negotiator walked directly to the admiral. Eye to eye, less than a meter apart, the Plentari supreme authority reminded everyone who was in charge.

"Admiral, you presume to know more than me. You believe your tactics cannot be questioned. Admiral, I will grant you one opportunity to respond correctly.

"You will deploy the forces as I have ordered. You will prepare your troops for the final sacrifice."

The admiral hesitated to respond. When she spoke, her tone was tart and her stance firm.

"Madame Negotiator, military tactics are my..."

The admiral did not finish her sentence. The ultimate Plentari authority pulled her micro-laser saber in one smooth arc and removed the truculent admiral's head. Not one head turn, nor eye glance, from the stoic Plentari at the sound of a severed head hitting the floor.

Stepping to her left, eye-to-eye with the second in command of the Plentari military, the Madame Negotiator waited for the vice-admiral to speak. The vice-admiral did not disappoint, responding in the tone of a competent, yet compliant, warrior.

"Sixty percent of our forces at the projected emergence point. Thirty percent halfway to the other emergence point. The remaining fighters are augmenting the planetary defenses.

"All troops ready for the final sacrifice."

"Excellent. Vice-Admiral, you are promoted to Admiral of the forces. Do not fail us."

"I will not fail, nor do I presume to know more than the Madame Negotiator.

"That is astute, Admiral. Why do you think it is important to make that statement?"

"I believe you must possess additional information about the attack."

"You are correct. Please, make ready."

"Yes, Madame Negotiator. A question if I may?"

Receiving the Plentari equivalent of a nod of confirmation, the admiral issued her query.

"The human adage?"

"Let this not be our last stand."

TC3, Executive Counsel

Chancellor Wilbon was staring at the British Five-Star General, who currently held the TC3 position of Space Command Commander.

"Can we do it?"

"I have no idea."

"What do you mean, you have no idea? It is

your JOB to KNOW and to have IDEAS. You have ten seconds to produce something."

When the general did not respond, Michelle turned to Admiral Joshua Turner, vice-chairman of the TC3.

"Admiral Turner, you commanded the *Hákarl* in battle. You have fought alongside the *Jaguar* and the *Dugr*, and you know Lucinda well. What is your assessment?"

After staring down the disappointing General, Admiral Turner, Josh, spoke to the table. Looking at each council member in turn, he spoke with a calm authority.

"The reason the second message was secured is that the crew of the *Dugr* believe it and want us to prepare. That is obvious. What is not obvious is what is not in the message.

"There are no suggested tactics. There are no summaries of their encounter with the Megvesnaith. They know something, and they are holding on to it until they are closer to home."

Ending, Josh knew what was coming next. Michelle did not disappoint.

"Speculate."

"Lucinda and Corb don't think we can defeat the Megvesnaith."

"Why not?"

"Either the Megvesnaith are too powerful, or there is something else. It is unlikely that we would not be able to hold our ground in a stand-up fight.

I am confident we could fight to a standstill until the *Dugr* returns. That leaves something else. Don't ask what that something might be. There are too many variables to form a conclusion."

"What do we do?"

"We do what the message says. We put our forces, all of them, at the emergence point and fight like hell to keep the Megvesnaith out of the Sol system."

"General, work with Admiral Turner to deploy our forces. No bogies get past our gauntlet."

"Madame Chairman, it is my opinion you are too inexperienced and frankly, too naïve, to make these decisions. I move for a vote of no confidence."

The General's sycophant who held the council seat designated for the TC3 Commerce Secretary could not second the motion quickly enough.

"Seconded!"

Michelle's smile unnerved the General. She turned to the one person everyone at the table respected.

"Davinder?"

"I am not permitted to make a motion. If I were permitted, I would move the motion of no confidence include a provision. Should the vote of no confidence be voted down, the General will resign his seat immediately."

Joshua's grin was broad. "I motion as such."

A chorus of seconds to the motion was a surprise to the pompous general. Michelle's smile compelled the General to break a sweat.

"Any other discussion? No? The motion is for a hand vote of no confidence in the Chancellor. All those in favor of no confidence signify by raising your right hand and stating 'aye.'"

Michelle's smile brightened.

"For the record, the count is two ayes. All those opposed to a vote of no confidence in the Chancellor, signify by raising your right hand and stating 'nay.'"

Michelle's face turned stern, her smile gone, she focused on the General and his sycophant.

"For the record, the count is thirteen nays, with one abstention. General, please exit the facility. Admiral Turner, you will assume the position of the commander of our defenses."

"Madame Chancellor, I request a mediator."

"General, you are still here? Sergeant at Arms, please escort the General from the facility. Do not let him back in his office. All of his access credentials are terminated. Put him on the street."

Two massive security guards forcibly grab the general, yanking him backward, toppling his plush conference room chair. Dragging and pushing him out of the conference room, the guards enjoyed humiliating the snobbish general. The acting Commerce Secretary chased along after the general.

"Jol?"

"Yes, Miss Wilbon?"

"I am Chancellor Wilbon. I want you to terminate the General's access to all TC3 related materials."

"Confirmed, all access revoked. Is there anything else?"

"No, Jol, thank you. As I was saying, Admiral Turner, you will assume the command of our defenses until the British leadership designates a replacement for the General.

"Jol?"

"Yes, Chancellor?"

"There is something else. I want you to run an analysis. Gather all the information available on the Megvesnaith. Correlate the information you gather with the messages we received from the *Dugr*. From the analysis, assess the probability of our capability to defend Sol successfully."

"Understood, the data collection and analysis will require time."

"How much time?"

"At least one hour."

Smiling at the silly concern from the AI, Michelle continued. "Jol, an hour for the analysis is not a concern. Please proceed. Do not distribute the results. Anything you conclude is Eyes Only for me, Admiral Turner, and General Khatter."

"General Khatter's security status was

reduced when he stepped down from the chancellorship."

"I see. Davinder, your retirement is going to be delayed a few days longer."

TC3 Chairman Emeritus, General Davinder Khatter, nodded affirmatively.

"Jol, General Khatter's security clearance is reinstated. Eyes only, you got that?"

"Yes, Chancellor."

"Davinder, I want your opinion."

"Josh is correct. There is something we do not know. We need to prepare, but …"

"But what?"

"It is not like Lucinda or Corb to hold back information."

"Agreed. What do you think it means?"

"Michelle, the *Dugr* thinks we are in trouble."

Dugr, Galley

Corb was ignoring his coffee. "Landry, how long before we can open the bi-directional micro-wormhole?"

"Corb, do you want to know when we can instantiate a point-to-point communication with Sol?"

"Yes, and a point-to-point with Plentari, and one with K'an."

"As you know, we cannot establish the link while we are in the trilateral domain. On our projected flight path, if we drop into standard space in seven hours, we should be able to contact a communications relay.

"Assuming the maps are accurate, and the relay is functional."

"Dad, why do you want to drop out of transit to send another message? Everyone must have received the first messages."

"Bonnie, using the micro-wormhole communications, we can create a link that is one-hundred percent secure."

"I understand. You want the information about the defensive plans to be secure. You want the details of our attack on the Megvesnaith carrier to be secret."

"Correct."

"What does it matter? The battle is coming. Let everyone stand to the fight."

"That is the Plentari academy influencing your thinking. We cannot let our understanding of the attack become public knowledge. We need to avoid widespread panic."

"You are protecting people who are incapable of accepting reality. You think you need to protect them from the truth."

"Yes, that, but more importantly, people need hope. People fight for many reasons, but two reasons always rise to the top.

"One reason is people fight to defend their home and family. None fight more bravely, are more willing to die for the cause than the warriors protecting their home and family.

"Second, people fight for a cause for which they have unbending beliefs.

"Warriors with an unbending belief, who are also defending their home and family, are to be feared."

"I do not understand. If what you say is true, tell everyone the details of the attack. Sharing the information will create warriors willing to die to protect their homeworld."

"Normally, that is the correct strategy. This is different."

"How is it different?"

In quiet personal contemplation, the first shift had been listening to Bonnie and Corb's discussion. Nick softly responded.

"Give me the strength to die well. William Wallace."

"Exactly, Nick. Bonnie, how did we destroy the Megvesnaith carrier?"

"We ruptured its antimatter containment field."

"Correct. How did we do that?"

Bonnie was beginning the see the problem.

"Essentially, we snuck up on the carrier and stabbed it in the side until it exploded."

"Right. Who else can sneak up on a carrier, through its ring of defensive fighters, then stab it in the side until it explodes?"

Bonnie stopped responding. Thinking, contemplating, when she spoke, her voice cracked.

"They can't win without us."

"No, they *can* win with the correct strategy."

"Dad?"

"I won't let anything happen to your mother. Davinder and Josh will not let anything happen to your mother."

Landry's avatar appeared over the sideboard.

"Yes, Landry?"

"Corb, it is time for you to replace Janish on the riser."

"Thank you. Bonnie, I want to talk to you about something. When my shift is over, let's have dinner in my cabin."

"Okay."

Bonnie watched the crew leave the galley. Like a bad dream, her thoughts kept returning to the same topic.

He knows something.
Something really big.
He wants me to know he is watching me.
He knows I have to do something.
No, he knows I will do whatever is required, and that makes him afraid.
I need to speak to JJ.
The answer is in the legends.

She does not turn away from her pain.
JJ will know.

Dugr, **Bridge**

"Landry, where are we?"

"Lucinda, we are very far from everything."

"Okay, smartass, did you connect to a communications relay?"

"Yes."

"Can you establish the micro-wormhole?"

"Yes, but I recommend receipt of the incoming transmissions before we respond."

"Transmissions?"

"Yes, the communication relay is indicating there are thousands of messages addressed to the *Dugr*."

"Thousands?"

"Eleven-thousand, eight-hundred, and seventy-eight."

"Holy moly. Download all of the messages. I want you to scan any that are not classified or encrypted. Categorize them by priority, source, and request."

"More than half are encrypted."

"Damn. Okay, scan everything. Categorize the message by priority, source, and request. We need to re-prioritize and narrow the list.

"Anything personal, from family or friends, is the lowest priority. Direct them appropriately.

Anything from a planetary governing council is a top priority. Anything related to military readiness, the second priority. For everything else, make an assessment and classify it based on the parameters.

"Download completed. Assessment is commencing. The estimate to complete is thirty-five minutes.

"Miss Wilbon?"

"Yes, Landry?"

"There is a priority one message from your mother."

"Thank you."

After receiving a nod of approval, Bonnie pulls over Cass's ever-present tablet. She reads the message, chuckles before looking up at her father.

"Mom says you better have some good news and, her words, 'Right the fuck now or you are going to have a problem when you get back to Earth.'"

Everyone's mood brightened.

"She sent that to you because she knows you won't let me slack. Lucinda is correct. First, we need Landry's assessment of the messages. Then we will agree on the best response."

Four hours into reading the categorized messages and trying to make sense of the thousands of requests, Nick's patience reached its endpoint.

"Jeez, Lucinda. Damn. Who knew good intentions could go sideways so quickly."

"Nick, that is an understatement. Landry, wake up the second shift, get them up here. While we wait, any good news?"

"Alva is growing like a weed. She knows *mor og far* are coming home soon."

Ragnar saved Cass from the odd looks of confusion.

"We are teaching Alva English and Norwegian. She knows mother and father are coming home soon."

The second shift files on to the bridge and assumes their now-familiar alternate seating. Lucinda begins the debrief.

"The messages are what you'd expect. Eighty-seven percent are a request for The Redeemer to protect a system or planet from the Megvesnaith.

"Eight percent are suggestions on how The Redeemer can defeat the Megves horde. Three percent are offers of payment to save some government or potentate or religious sect from being made irrelevant by the Megves scum.

"Two-hundred and twelve messages, about one-point-eight percent, are legitimate requests from governmental authorities. Many of the claims are redundant. Twenty-nine systems are requesting our assistance.

"Twenty-three of the messages are re-classified as priority one and require our attention. Landry, scroll the priority one messages, in the order I listed, with the highlights I requested."

The combined crew read the messages, read the highlights, one after the other until the list was exhausted. It was Bonnie who spoke first.

"Landry, please put up message number eleven. Yep, that is the correct message. The TC3 is doing what you told them. They want to know how to defeat the Megvesnaith. Can they defeat the Megvesnaith?"

Corb understood the question was an indirect request to open up about his planning.

"Yes, but they do not know how."

"Are you going to tell them?"

"Yes, it is in my message to your mother."

After the pause, JJ spoke.

"Landry, message number six, please. Thank you. The Plentari are prepared and will not be defeated. The Madame Negotiator has determined the correct strategy to defend Plentari. Is it our mission to assist Plentari?"

JJ had pointed his formal request at Lucinda.

"No, that is one of the topics we need to discuss. Please hold that discussion for a few minutes. We need to agree on several items before we send the information. Anyone else? Janish, you look concerned."

"The Ch'en. Landry, message number two,

please. There, line seven, they are offering anything to protect K'an. We have known them for decades. Not once have they offered to trade anything with no conditions.

"Do I trust them? Not hardly. But the request cannot be ignored. According to the request, they are unable to defend themselves. Corb?"

"Janish, your concerns are noted. I think we agree. The planet K'an and the Ch'en people are the most vulnerable of the projected targets. Unfortunately for the Ch'en, they are not at the top of our list of friends to help.

"Nick, you are surprisingly quiet. What are you thinking?"

"Landry, message number seventeen, please."

Instead of speaking to the message and the highlighted passages, Nick glared at Corb, forcing him to talk first.

"What do you think it means?"

"I think you sent that fat fook-wad Commodore Jexond on a mission. What did you promise him?"

Radiating a cheerful glow, a bright smile, with crystal blue eyes glimmering, Corb loved his friends.

"Promise? I promised him nothing."

"Nothing? That is a bunch of bull-sod."

"No, really, nothing."

"Arg. I will bite. What did you tell him?"

"I told him a lie."

Everyone perked up at Corb's comment.

"A lie?"

"Yes, Nick. A lie. I told him if he did not respect the vow of loyalty, I would let it be known The Redeemer considered the Ajawlil untrustworthy."

"You extorted his support?"

"I sure did."

"Just when I thought there was nothing new to learn about our little Corb. Go figure. I remember when you were younger than Bonnie. That Corb, way back then, was not nearly smart enough to successfully buy beer, get a girl, let alone extort a Commodore."

Corb piled on. "Nick, that Corb didn't know his arse from a hole in the ground."

The snickering died quickly. Nick continued.

"Where did you send our friend, the Commodore?"

"Landry scroll the responses Lucinda and I created. Some of the responses will affect our decision making. We will vote on each of the first five.

"Do not be confused. Lucinda has the authority to issue these as orders. However, our decisions will affect this crew. Therefore ... Lucinda?"

"Corb is correct. Unless there is a strong

objection and an alternative suggestion, the messages go. I want to be clear: You do not get to object because you don't like it. If you object, you have to provide an alternative. Understood?"

Lucinda looked to each crewman, receiving a confirmation of understanding.

"Great, message one."

The crew read the message. When everyone is looking at everyone else, Nick's wry humor emotes.

"You could have eased us into reality."

"Any objections? None? Landry, send it. Estimated time of arrival?"

"Earth will receive the message in three hours and twelve minutes. It will arrive at Q'eqchi. The security detail will know what to do with the secured message."

"Message two, please."

JJ summarized the message with Bonnie's support. "Plentari is making ready for the defense of the coming attack. The Madame Negotiator understood the threat and has made arrangements."

"JJ is correct. The Plentari will not be defeated."

"Any objections? None? Landry, send it. Message number three, please."

"So that is what you did with fat fook-wad Commodore Jexond."

"Yes, Nick. Two birds, one stone."

Corey, who was quiet, seldom speaking after the broken nose incident, asked a soft question to which Corb eagerly responded.

"Two birds?"

"Yes, Corey. You are aware. The Ch'en are back-stabbing scum. The First are the race that put this all into motion three millennia ago. When the First died off and stopped manipulating the galaxy, with support from the Xjaal, the Ch'en stepped in and began controlling entire races of people. They took a particular interest in screwing with humans.

"The Ch'en conspired with the Xjaal for control of the galaxy. When I came along, they conspired to control me. They failed and are now ... now they are worried.

"The Ch'en are afraid, and their fear translates to an increase in the hate their culture already possessed. Hatred for two things: Artificial intelligence and clones. They have legends and lore that foretell of Ch'en subjugation by machines and creatures who do not possess a soul.

"Sending the Ajawlil to defend K'an is a little bit of payback. If the Ajawlil are successful, the Ch'en will owe the clones a substantial debt.

"If they are not successful in destroying the Megvesnaith, the Ch'en will be subjugated. Either way, the Ch'en Harmony will never be the same.

"Bird one, I get the Ajawlil a permanent assignment to protect K'an. Bird two, the Ch'en leadership, will know I did this as payback."

Corey sat in dumbfounded silence.

NT chimed. "Nick was right. Our Corb is all grown up and badass."

Bonnie was not having it. "Extortion? Payback? Is that why we are out here?"

Lucinda stepped over Corb's response.

"No, that is NOT why we are out here. What you are experiencing is what the TC3 has learned, what humans are learning. Sadly, only those who have been in deep space utterly understand what is required. General Khatter, Admiral Turner, your Mother, and a few others understand.

"Human values and conditional actions have little or no benefit out here. The trade missions, the commerce negotiations, act as if there are values common between the sentient races. The idea of universal values is a façade. Each species has its morals and ethos. Humans are infantile on the interstellar stage, but we are quick learners.

"Out here, we have played, we are playing now, and we will continue to play by the rules *we* set."

Turning to eye Beth, Corey, JJ, and ending on Bonnie, Lucinda closed the topic.

"You do not have to agree. You do not have to like our decisions. But note this, and do not forget. Out here, the rules are made by those who can enforce them."

Corb waited, then continued.

"Any objections? None? Landry, send it, and

put up message number eight."

The message was surprising in its simplicity. Addressed to the planetary leaders of the five systems Landry determined had the highest probability of attack, the message left no doubt about the requirements for survival.

MEGVESNAITH INVASION FORCE
DEFENSE STRATEGY

DO NOT LET THE MEGVESNAITH IN-SYSTEM
DESTROY THE CARRIER AT EMERGENCE

The Megvesnaith will attack using biological subjugation. The release of the biological subjugation agent will result in all life being eliminated or absorbed by the Megvesnaith.

Destroy the attacking carrier by disrupting its antimatter containment field.

The attached video is the destruction of one Megvesnaith invasion carrier.

Use the accompanying carrier profile specifications to develop your attack plan to compromise and rupture the invasion carrier's antimatter containment field.

No other options are viable.

It was Cass who broke the somber silence. "Lucinda, do you think they can do it? Will they do it?"

"If you mean the TC3, yes. My guess is Admiral Turner will lead the mission himself.

"If you mean Plentari, yes. I am sure there is a long line of attack fighter pilots volunteering.

"If you mean the Ch'en, no. Corb's plan to send the Ajawlil to the K'an system is their only hope.

"The other targets ... I have no idea."

Turning to Corb, Lucinda was silently asking for his encouragement. The tone of Corb's response was uncertain.

"I have an idea."

Bonnie was focused on her father, her thoughts returning and revolving again like a bad dream on repeat.

His connection is bright.
He is beaming.
He knows something.
Something really big.
He wants me to know he is watching me.
He knows I will do something.

JJ.
The answer is in the legends.
JJ will know.

Part Three

Destinies can be altered.

Death to All, Bridge

"Commodore, we have received a message. It is marked for you."

The Commodore did not bother to get up from the reclining chaise in his ready room. Waving away the communications officer, his pudgy hand pulled down the monitor. Round fingers pressing the icons, he read the message, reviewed its attachments, and like a walrus sliding off the ice sheet into the sea, he slipped off the chaise toward the bridge.

"Report"

"Commodore, we are twenty-two minutes from entry. There is one transit to complete. We will be in the K'an system in fifteen hours."

"XO, if the attacking forces have beaten us to the system, we will chase them down and engage immediately. Otherwise, when we emerge, all stop.

"It is likely we are ahead of the attacking forces. After we achieve all stop, position us point-five lightyears from the emergence point.

"Deploy all fighters using attack formations Gamma-One and Delta-Two. Colonel Jednira and his Alpha squadron will lead the attack.

"Mission brief in one hour. I am ordering Jednira and all of Alpha Squadron to attend the mission brief."

"Confirming your orders, Commodore. Deploy all fighters?"

"Yes, XO, all fighters. There is no alternative plan. We will destroy the enemy carrier."

"Understood."

K'an, Planetary Council Meeting

The three Ch'en High-Council members and two former council members are debating the messages received from the *Dugr*.

"He has overstepped. He cannot do this."

"He can, and he did."

"We can't let this stand."

"Do you have an alternative? Is there another way?"

"How do we know the attackers are coming here? These directions are a plan to control K'an and our people. This is a plan to disrupt the Harmony."

"If you had not noticed, vice-chairman, there is rioting in the streets. There has been growing opposition to our leadership since the enforced isolation. The Harmony is in danger of being broken beyond repair. How is a new threat going to make it worse?"

"Enough. We accept the terms. We have no alternative. We accept the terms today. Tomorrow we will alter the arrangement."

"How will we alter the agreement?"

"I do not know, but we will not let the soulless put their feet on K'an. The soulless will never rule the Ch'en."

TC3, Executive Counsel

"Michelle, do we have a choice?"

"No, Josh, we do not. I guess you were accurate, Davinder. The *Dugr* did not want this information widely known. They were correct in waiting to send a secure communication. Any further debate?"

No one spoke. No one looked Michelle or Josh in the eye. They were about to vote to send people to their death.

"All in favor, raise your right hand ... For the

record, the vote is unanimous."

Michelle and the other TC3 council members stood to leave. When Michelle hesitated, everyone stopped moving.

"Davinder ..."

"Michelle, it is the correct choice."

Turning to Admiral Turner, the longtime trio of friends, Davinder, Michelle, and Josh, had an unspoken understanding. Michelle's lips quivered as she spoke.

"Josh, good hunting."

Dugr, Corb's Cabin

"Dad, do you think Earth will be okay?"

"You remind me of your mother."

"You are avoiding my question. Do you think Earth will be okay?"

"I do not know. We have been successful before. We will find a way this time too."

"Wishes and hope? That is not encouraging."

"Do you want the truth, or should I paint a rosy picture for you?"

Bonnie paused and considered.

"Truth. Why did you ask me here? You said you wanted to talk about something."

"I do, but first I have a question. Before the training, before your time at the Plentari Military Academy, you were different. You were bubbly.

"Always talking and always laughing. Now,

you only speak when someone speaks to you. You seldom ask questions. We miss your smile. Bonnie ... Bunny, what happened at the training academy?"

Aalborinn, Bonnie, did not expect the question. Corb remained quiet, forcing his daughter to respond.

"We talked about Plentari training. Mother, you, and me, we agreed. You know, we decided it was my choice. Why are you asking? What is the point of your question? It does not matter. I will tell you what you want to know. The first two, maybe two- and a half years, were severe. For more than a millennium, only Plentari have attended the academy. No other races are considered worthy of the Plentari warrior training. I was the first non-Plentari to attend and the first to graduate.

"The Madame Negotiator put these on me."

Bonnie slid her sleeve up, showing the three colored marks.

"I was told no Madame Negotiator had ever conferred the title on a graduate ...

"It was her way of telling the Plentari their society is changing. There were a lot of Plentari who disapprove of a foreigner attending the academy ..."

Bonnie pauses, thinking.

Plentari, Training Academy

The first meal was usually a time for conversation as well as the trainees getting to know each other. Always sitting by herself for two months, Bonnie endured a parade of trainees walking behind her and bumping her on their way by the seated alien. Yanking on the back of her tunic or tugging on her short curly hair. Each with something vile to say.

"You have no fur. You will not survive the week."

"Brown hair, brown skin, no fur. I will enjoy giving you pain in our Contest."

"No fur. You are not worthy."

"Your death will not be mourned and quickly forgotten."

"Humans cover themselves because they are embarrassed. They have no fur."

Pushed to the edge by the stream of insults, Bonnie let the trainees know she would not go away quietly. In one motion, she grabbed her food tray, swinging it in an arc. Augmented by her telekinetic abilities, she smashed the next trainee across the face before the trainee could bump into her or issue an insult.

Standing over the prone trainee, Bonnie tore the tunic from her shoulders, looked around the dining hall, and stared down the room before departing for her quarters.

Dugr, Corb's Cabin

"The other trainees thought I did not belong. They thought I was admitted to the academy because I am your daughter. They thought I was not tough enough to be a Plentari warrior."

"You fought?"

"Every day, for a couple of years."

"Bonnie ... I don't know what to say."

"Why should you say anything? It was my choice. I wanted to attend. Being your daughter got me in, but being tough kept me in."

"I thought the legends foretold..."

Bonnie cut off her father's sentence.

"Yeah, there is that. Why did you ask me here? Did you want to know about the training? It was tough."

"You fought _every_ day?"

"Yes."

"Did any other trainees fight every day?"

"They call it the Contest. You can challenge any other trainee to the Contest. It is simple. Hand to hand battle. The weaker trainees receive frequent challenges. Get tough or get out."

"Get out?"

"I know you think the only way out is to graduate or death. That is not true. Not anymore. You are permitted to request to leave. No one asks.

To the Plentari, quitting the training is a scarlet letter. Quitting is a shame on a level unknown to humans.

"If a Plentari were chosen to attend the academy, then chose to leave, they would have to leave the planet. They would be shunned."

"How many died?"

"A few, but you are asking how many did I kill? Other than the assassins. One. Killing her did not stop the requests for the Contest. It took a while, but I figured it out."

Bonnie paused, considering.

"Dad, when you were young, younger than I am now, did you kill a woman in Waxahachie?"

"I did. The woman was a religious zealot who was holding a gun to your mother's head. She wanted to kill me. It was ... Necessary."

"That is the point. Sometimes it is necessary. What I did not understand was the nature of the problem. Why was it necessary to fight every day? I fought because I did not understand the Plentari culture or the nuances of their racial bias. Systemic prejudice is the origin of their abusive nature. The challenges are xenophobic bullshit.

"But that was not it."

Pausing again, this time she looked at her father with the question.

"How do you live with it? Killing someone? Death?"

Corb did not miss a beat.

"Like you, I ignore it. We are here for a reason. We have these gifts for a reason. I stopped questioning it a long time ago. After Rýma, what we learned there, I no longer worry about what has passed. I worry about what is next and how I can make Earth a better place."

"Rýma?"

"Forget I said that name. Please, never repeat it to anyone. There are things there ... If anyone finds it, the entire galaxy will be in trouble."

"Okay. You said I am not bubbly. I am the same, just older."

"No, you are not the same. You think differently. Some of it is about getting older, wiser. But ... I think you heard the legends. I think you are worried the legends will come true."

He knows!
How does he know?
Be cool.
Find out what The Redeemer knows.

"Legends?"

Corb laughed before responding.

"You can't fool me. I saw your connection flare. You heard about the legends, and you think they apply to you."

"What makes you think they don't?"

"Because I know what happened with the

Contests."

"You don't know. What do you *think* happened?"

"You used your powers to defeat everyone. One day you realized, the other trainees wanted you to fight as a Plentari. Fight the Contest without your powers. That is the day everything changed."

"How do you know all that?"

"Jirxena."

"The Counselor?"

"She is not just a counselor."

"Son of a bitch."

"Exactly. Jirxena, and JJ's mother, Jirmina, were part of the crew of the *Jaguar*. They were members of the Madame Negotiator's Imperial Guard. They volunteered to join the crew of the *Jaguar* to fight the Xjaal.

"When we returned, Jirxena was promoted to the Commander of the Imperial Guard. She took the temporary role of Counselor to keep an eye on you.

"She is back to leading the Imperial Guard."

"I thought I saw the stripes once ... What did Jirxena tell you?

"She said the day you figured it out was the day the trainees began to think of you as an equal."

"I guess."

"No guessing, it is true. Do you believe the legend?"

Bonnie stared long and hard at her father.

Unsure, she gave the only answer she knew to be true.

"Yes."

"Good. Landry prep the galley. Bonnie and I will have dinner in ten minutes.

"Confirmed."

"Bonnie, I have one more question. Buffy the Vampire Slayer?"

"What can I say? It was a good move."

Dugr, Bonnie's Cabin

"JJ, thank you for coming."

"Is it permitted for me to be in your cabin?"

"Yes, and stop being a prude. This is a human ship. You know humans allow males and females to be alone together, to share quarters. Sit down."

While JJ pulls the desk chair around, Bonnie pulls down her tunic, making her stripes visible. The male Plentari is unfazed at Bonnie's bare chest, but his heritage makes him uncomfortable being alone with a female.

"I understood graduates receive one stripe. They confer two stripes on exceptional warriors. You received three stripes. The highest order. Is it true the Madame Negotiator herself put them on you?"

"Yes, that is true."

"Is it also true you were undefeated in the

Contest?"

"That is also true."

"One more question, if I may?"

"Yes."

"Is it true you fought the Contest every day and that you killed Jaderna?"

"You know of Jaderna?"

"Jaderna was known to all Plentari. She was not easily defeated. Before the academy, she and her sister fought in the Contests for credits. When the academy rules changed, allowing more Plentari to apply for admittance, she was the first selected.

"Before the rules changed, Jaderna was of a class not worthy of being a Plentari warrior."

"I did not know that about Jaderna. Yes, I fought every day until the third year. Yes, in the contest, I killed Jaderna and severely wounded her sister."

"You received no honor in killing Jaderna?"

"Correct. I received no honor because I used my powers. The Plentari consider using the powers to be a cheat. There is no honor in being a cheat. I defeated her sister, Jadexna, without using my powers."

"You are truly Plentari. Aalborinn, Daughter of the Redeemer, First Daughter of the Plentari."

"They gave me that title before I entered the training."

"Yes, but the important thing is you kept the title."

"I did."

"Why did you ask me here?"

"Do you know of the legend of Aalborinn and the Seekers of Blood?"

"You ask about something that is for children who misbehave. If the child does not correct the bad behavior, the Seekers of Blood will take them for the alter."

"I am aware. Do you know the legend?"

"Yes, I know the legend. Why do you ask me? Aalborinn, you can search the records. Landry can provide information to help your search."

"Because I know something about you."

Archetypal Plentari, JJ refused to move or appear shocked.

"I know you studied Plentari History and Lore. You learned to interpret the legends from the Elders, from the Saga. You are the first male to be given the full history of the Plentari."

"How do you know this?"

"Do you know who my mother is?"

"Yes, she is The Redeemer's mate."

"Don't ever say that to her! But yes, she is that. She is also the Chancellor of the TC3. That means she might be the most powerful woman on Earth. Do you know why you are on this ship?"

"I was selected from the candidates."

"That selection process was planned to mask choosing you over a female. Your knowledge of Plentari history pushed you to the top of the selection list.

"You were chosen because you know the legends."

Realizing he is a pawn in the big game, JJ refuses to concede.

"I was selected. I bested the others."

"Sure, that's what we will go with, because why not? Now, tell me about the legend of Aalborinn and the Seekers of Blood."

Dugr, Bridge

The tension in Lucinda's voice is thick.

"Landry report."

"Captain, the revised trajectory was accurate. We are equidistant to Earth, Plentari, and K'an. I was able to ping a celestial beacon. I have confirmed, due to the time dilation effect of the slipstream, we lost three days in transit before we started using the trilateral slipstream.

"I pulled the messages from the communications relay. Do you want a summary?"

"Yes, please."

"Earth has marshaled all ships in the Sol system, including any lite freighters, and are positioning the flotilla at the emergence point. Admiral Turner is personally leading the defense force from the *Hákarl*.

"There are private messages from the elder

Miss Wilbon for you, for Corb, and Miss Wilbon."

"Landry, call me Aalborinn or Bonnie."

"Yes, Bonnie. Captain, the Plentari have called up all reserves. Any ship that can fly is en route to the defense coordinates. The Madame Negotiator ordered their forces divided. Sixty percent at the emergence point projected to be the first arrival point. She placed thirty percent of the attack forces half-way between Plentari and the second hyper-tunnel emergence point. Ten percent of the fighter forces held back to augment the planetary defenses.

"Captain, I recommend another message to Plentari. They must not allow the Megvesnaith carrier to begin dispersing their weapon.

"Agreed, resend the warning message, and add the emphasis. Put Corb's name, along with mine, on the new message. Continue the message brief."

"Commodore Jexond confirmed receipt of the messages and reports he will be ready. The Commodore reports *The Death to All*'s arrival in the K'an system is approximately two hours from now.

"There is something else.

"Something missing from the data."

"Landry, it is not like you to hesitate. Is this a new personality algorithm?"

"No, Captain, I am just trying to express concern and worry better."

"Worry? Can an AI worry? Is worry possible?

What are you *worried* about?"

"Captain, none of the sensor logs, at any of the systems along the designated flight paths report Megvesnaith carriers. The monitor buoys in three of the five transit systems between the hyper-tunnels report no activities. There should be reports of the five carriers emerging on the projected pathways, transiting the systems between hyper-tunnels, then entry into the next hyper-tunnel.

"The sensors report no Megvesnaith activity."

"None?"

"Captain, the sensors are working correctly. They are reporting other activities."

"Hypothesis."

"Either our analysis was in error, or when we destroyed carrier Charlie, the Megvesnaith changed their strategy."

Bonnie is listening, but her mind wanders to something she read while at the academy.

Plentari, Training Academy

"Aalborinn, read this, and tomorrow we will discuss its message."

"Counselor, this is an ancient scroll. Am I permitted to read something so dear to the Plentari?"

"You are permitted what I tell you is

permitted."

"Counselor, this is a book of tales and legends. I do not understand."

"Read all of the stories. You must try to absorb the story titled: Aalborinn and the Seekers of Blood."

"Counselor, I do not understand."

"Aalborinn, you have seen the future?"

"I have seen one future. There is no assurance our actions today will not change the future."

"Do you ignore your Second Sight?"

"No, counselor, but I understand the future is not yet written. Every action taken or not taken changes the path of all futures. Some actions are small changes. Some actions are compounded and can change the course of the present and the future. The future is a history not yet written."

"Yes, I understand. Humans have a saying for what you describe. Do you know the saying?"

"Yes, it is referred to as The Butterfly Effect. The small wind created by a butterfly can grow into a storm."

"Aalborinn, *you* are the butterfly."

"Counselor, butterflies are fragile and easily eaten by birds."

"And some butterflies are fierce and powerful."

Dugr, **Bridge**

"Either way, the analysis was in error, or the Megvesnaith changed their strategy. I know you ran a bazillion scenarios to arrive at a new summary. What is the result of the new analysis?"

"Captain, you are correct. I was able to run a new analysis. The results are concerning."

"Landry, I don't like the new you. Stop with the hemming and hawing. Give me the report right now."

"The Megvesnaith have altered what we projected was their attack strategy. It is likely they have agreed to a rendezvous where they will reassess their plan."

"Did your analysis conclude where the rendezvous is going to occur?"

The monitors changed before Landry continued. "It is likely occurring in the system displayed. This system is a barren quadrant the Plentari refer to as Zeon-One-Alpha-Eighty-One. It is in deep space and is an intersection. There are five hyper-tunnel endpoints in this system. There are no functioning communication relays in the system."

"An intersection of five hyper-tunnel endpoints and no comms relay nodes? Why not?"

"It appears the communications relay node went offline thirty-seven hours ago. It is likely the carrier we designated Delta arrived at the intersection approximately thirty-seven hours ago."

"Damn. What about the attack group headed to Earth?"

Morphing the video images, Landry continued. "The communications nodes traced their entry here. The intersection relay reporting their last location is two hyper-tunnel segments from Sol.

"However, there is no report of their exiting the intersection."

"They are waiting for something."

"That is the most likely conclusion."

Using her nanobots to connect to the *Dugr*, ignoring Landry's typical role, Lucinda issued a ship-wide announcement. "All hands, report to the bridge."

"Captain, the second shift is asleep."

"Landry, I do not care. Wake them and get them up here. Corb, your recon idea was a good one. We need a new plan."

Corb nodded acceptance. The first shift sat quietly, waiting for Beth, Corey, and JJ.

Dugr, Bridge

"I am sorry to drag you out of bed, but this is important. Our original analysis was flawed, or the Megvesnaith changed their strategy.

"Landry, repeat what your new analysis indicates."

"It is likely the Megvesnaith are mustering to consolidate forces. Because we were successful in destroying carrier Charlie, they are changing their master plan.

"Captain, the probability of a change in the master plan for their conquest is extremely high. However, the expected results of their new planning effort are unknown."

"What do you mean, unknown? There are a few options available. They have five carrier groups. One, designated Alpha, is approaching the Sol system but has stopped awaiting instructions. The other carrier groups are holed-up in the middle of nowhere.

"Landry, what are the *high probability* results of the analysis?"

"Captain, based on the available datum, the Megvesnaith are consolidating forces. They will combine their carriers into battle groups and attack a fewer number of targets."

Lucinda was nodding, almost bobbing her head in deep thought. The others watched, waited, wondering. Bonnie took on a thousand-mile stare.

Nona's, Salon

Ten-year-old Bonnie is pestering her great-grandmother.

"Nona, why do you call it the salon?"

"The salon is where proper people sit and discuss the day's events. Proper people do not call it a living room."

"When will mother return?"

"Why are you asking questions for which you already have the answers? What is bothering you, child?"

"Nona, I had a dream."

"A dream? Tell me about your dream."

"It was a dream, but I was not asleep. It was a dream in my head."

"That is what we call the Sight, what others call the Second Sight. Tell me, what did you see in your head?"

"I saw myself. I was older. I was on a ship. A spaceship. I had to do something bad."

"Bad?"

"Yes, I had to do something bad to save people."

"Saving people is not bad."

"No, Nona, I had to do something bad to other people to save our people."

"Are you saying you saved Earth?"

"I don't know. It was hard to tell. The bad people were not nice. They wanted to live here. I saved everyone."

"Have you heard of the bad people? Have you seen them before? Maybe it is just your imagination."

"No, I checked."

"How did you check?"

"I asked Jol."

"Honey, what did you do?"

"I used my mother's communication device. I know how to use the device in her office. I asked Jol, the artificial person on the space station, to help me. He told me he found a story about my dream."

"Tell me the story."

"I can't."

"Why not?"

"Because if I tell you, it will come true."

"I see ... In the story, do you save the world?"

"Not me, someone named Aalborinn. Aalborinn is a girl. She is a strong warrior."

"I see. Because the warrior in the story has a different name, you think it is someone else?"

"Yes. Maybe. I don't know. I am confused."

"Honey, there is no need to worry. The Sight often gives us things we do not understand. Give it some time. It will be made clear. Maybe you are seeing something that will happen to someone else. Maybe Aunt Lucinda or maybe Aunt Janish."

"Maybe. The girl in my dream was dark-skinned. Not dark like you. Sort of dark, like me. Maybe it is Aunt Janish ..."

"Bonnie, this is the Sight. This is what happens. Sometimes, in the Sight, you do not see the whole story. Next time you have the Sight, you tell me right away. We will figure it out together."

"Nona, does my dream, my Sight, mean you no longer have the Sight?"

"No, honey, I still have the Sight. But, like it has done in the before, it moved from my Nona to me. My Second Sight is moving to you. It is our blood. Honey Chili, I will help you understand its power.

"Now, I need a nap. Wake me for supper."

Dugr, Bridge

Bonnie is back in the present, listening to Lucinda. "Corb, Cass, didn't we read about something like this in the records... In the information we found?"

Corb is nodding at Lucinda's question, considering. Cass is frantically sliding icons on her tablet, looking for data. Landry jumps in.

"Captain, you did not ask me, but the answer is yes, sort of."

"Damn it. 'sort of' is not an answer? I am sure I do not like the new Landry. What did you find?"

"In one of the earliest files, there is a reference to the First orchestrating a genocidal battle between two cultures on a planet. A planet we call Megves Major."

Cass erupts.

"Got it! He is correct. We cataloged the entry then ignored it because Megves Major is so far out on the spur. Oh ... This is interesting ..."

Cass stopped to read, ignoring the fact the crew was listening to her. Eventually, Ragnar prodder her back to the present.

"Earth to Cass? Come in, Cass."

"Sorry. One of the professors assigned to assess the data we brought back wrote a summary of this entry. Not a summary exactly. He correlated the First and their creating the battle for supremacy on Megves Major with Robert Rynsburger ..."

Looking at Lucinda, NT interrupted Cass. "Wow, that is a name we have not heard in a long, long time."

Lucinda was part of the team that assassinated the owner of Morningstar Pharmaceuticals, Robert Rynsburger. She provided a brief history.

"Robert Rynsburger created Morningstar Pharmaceuticals to develop a cure for the cold and flu. He hired Baruti A. Wolmarans. Together, they cured the common cold and influenza virus. We think, we know, the Ch'en manipulated Wolmarans' data, which allowed him to develop the compound. He was successful, but that was not enough. The real intent of the product, called Coldstar, was to kill three-quarters of humanity. Rynsburger and Wolmarans wanted to wipe out six-billion people.

"Cass, what does that have to do with Megves Major and the First?"

"Lucinda, the professor made an assertion: The Ch'en are likely to emulate the First. He theorizes … wait … here it is:

'In the absence of a singular governing body, the interstellar capable galactic sentients will continue to compete for control and supremacy.

…

Where the original Overlords, the First, were evil and manipulative, they were equally benevolent in maintaining order and harmony throughout the galaxy.

Humans, their trading and mutual-defense partners, must remain vigilant in the pursuit of galactic harmony. Where the First were capable of putting down rebellions, the absence of a controlling body will foment thoughts and acts of rebellion and disobedience.

…

This analysis's summary conclusion is that new, more reliable defense treaties are necessary to ensure Earth's safety.

…

It would be wise for the TC3 to continue to seek,

or enhance, military defense alliances with the Plentari, the Ajawlil of the planet Zerain (formerly known as Gowah), and the Garune of the planet Kripkeni.'

There is more, but those are the relevant points."

Cass looked up, focused on Corb.

"No mention of the Ch'en, but this smells like their work. We have seen the dead planet, which means the Megvesnaith are desperate. I am not ruling out the Ch'en have some part in this little mess."

Ragnar's tone was terse. "Probably the Xjaal also."

"Yes, Ragnar, the Xjaal Council wants to restart their factories before the few remaining Xjaal are gone. This is important. We have no facts to prove any of this is accurate. We still have to decide what to do about the Megvesnaith."

Bonnie has another memory triggered by the conversation.

Nona's, Kitchen

Nona and Bonnie are seated at the kitchen breakfast table. Michelle is cooking and serving brunch. Both of the older women notice Bonnie was not her talkative self.

"Michelle, when do you have to return to Q'eqchi?"

"Nona, not for a few days. Bonnie, is something bothering you?"

"No, Mother."

"Are you sure?"

"Yes."

Bonnie was watching her great-grandmother. Frail and slight, the older woman realized what was wrong with the child. Sitting up straight, looking at the child, she said three words.

"You are lying."

The harsh tone caused Michelle to look up from her cooking. Bonnie could not look at her Nona.

"I am not."

"Yes, child, you are, and I will not have lying in my house ... You had another dream? You had some Sight?"

Bonnie's dower face immediately brightened.

"Yes."

"Do you want to tell me about it?"

"No."

"Why not?'

"Because it is bad."

"Bad like the other time? When you told me before?"

"No ... Worse."

"Worse?"

As Michelle puts the food plates down, her grandmother, Bonnie's great-grandmother, understood the problem.

"You saw my funeral."

Tears blocking her vision and unable to speak, Bonnie can only nod agreement.

"Baby, that is not something over which you should be crying. I may leave this life, but I will always be with you. In your heart. Come here, hug Nona."

Bonnie hugs her Nona. Michelle grips her child's arm. When Bonnie can breathe evenly again, Nona continues.

"Bonnie, I know you are sad. I know you did not want to see it. I know that you know, you will see a lot of things that will make you woeful and unhappy.

"Do not be sad. Wilbon women are strong. It is who we are. Strong women. We always have been. We always will be.

"You have the Sight. My Nona told me her sight would pass to me when she moved on. When I move on, you will receive my Sight. It has been the way of the Wilbon women since before they brought our ancestors to the Americas.

"You need to be strong. You need to be a Wilbon woman. Can you do that? Can you be strong for Nona?"

"Yes."

Bonnie was hugging her Nona tightly.

Michelle thought her daughter's tight hug might harm the frail woman.

Nona's, Kitchen – The Next Morning

Bonnie's tone is a matter of fact. No crack in her voice. No tears. No outward remorse. A strong Wilbon woman.

"Mother, Nona passed in the night."

Dugr, Bridge

"Captain, I have an idea. Well, a thought, maybe not an idea …"

Surprising everyone, the Plentari, who only spoke when spoken to, had volunteered to contribute.

"JJ, anything you have may help. Please, tell us."

"Captain, I believe the Megvesnaith are consolidating their forces. They have determined we can defeat a single carrier. Also, they know they are vulnerable at hyper-tunnel entry and emergence points.

"If they consolidate their fleet, they can improve the prospect of their attacks.

"They are going to sacrifice one of the carriers to get a second carrier through a system's defenses."

Cass expressed confusion. "JJ, they have

five carrier battle groups. One near Sol and four sitting in deep space."

"Yes, they have five carrier groups. They will send two carriers toward their primary target. The lone carriers will attempt to conquer the weaker targets."

Nick was skeptical. "There's a lot of ifs, buts, and assumptions in your theory."

"Yes, that is true. But it does not make the theory invalid."

Corb's tone was even in his question. "What makes you think this is their new strategy?"

"Redeemer, it is what I would do."

"Why would you change your plans?"

"The human General Sun Tzu said: 'The supreme art of war is to subdue the enemy without fighting.' That is what the Megvesnaith do. They use their biologics to subdue their target.

"Their goal is to get one of their carriers through the emergence from the hyper-tunnel transit. One invasion carrier is enough to release its weapon upon the system they are trying to conquer. When they release the bioweapon, they run and wait.

"Eventually, the leaders in the target system will concede. That is the Megvesnaith plan. Consolidating their fleet, sacrificing a carrier to achieve the goal is the price."

Corb understood JJ was correct. "It is not a field of a few acres of ground, but a cause, that we are defending, and whether we defeat the enemy in one battle, or by degrees, the consequences will be the same. Thomas Paine.

"The Megvesnaith plan to win by degrees. JJ, I think you are correct. Landry, take JJ's summary into account and run new scenarios. If they consolidate, how will they consolidate, and what are the likely targets?"

"Working."

"Lucinda, we need to make a choice."

"Yes, we do. We will wait for Landry's analysis, then decide. Nick, move us and make us a hole."

Nick turned to his console and pressed the three correct icons. The *Dugr* jumped to a new location two lightyears from their previous position. "Stealth mode activated."

"Landry?"

"Captain, we are a hole in space. Passive scanning initiated."

"Everyone, I know you have a lot to say ... Right now, we are going to take a break. Everyone stands down for a few hours. We are changing our clock. When we reconvene, we will call it oh-six hundred. Meet for breakfast, and we will discuss our options.

"Ladies, we need a break. A mental and physical break. Will you join me for some yoga?"

***Dugr*, Main Cargo Hold**

The women are sitting Indian style on their mats. Sweat slowly evaporating from the workout, the holographic yoga instructor silently waiting.

"This is pretty nice. Mats. Towels. Music. Real tea. No men. I like it. "

"Yes, Bonnie, it is one of the perks I insist on maintaining. I like to create breaks in the routine. Traveling in spaceships is boring, repetitive, and highly stressful on the good days. Yoga breaks the monotony. Also, boys are icky."

When the giggles and agreements subsided, Lucinda returned to the elephant in the room.

"I want your opinions. I will ask the men also, but right now, I want to know your thoughts. Beth, what do you think about our little problem?"

"Lucinda, I think JJ is correct. The Megvesnaith need to consolidate their power and try to get through the ambushes they know are waiting for them to stumble on. Simple."

"Janish?"

"I think they are going to try an end-run. Send two carriers to a single system and enter from two points. Entry from two points will increase their opportunity for success and maybe lose one but not both carriers."

"That is an excellent point. Landry?"

Landry's avatar replaced the yoga instructor.

"Yes, Lucinda?"

"Augment your tactical analysis. If the Megvesnaith send two carriers to one system, which systems have two entry points and are closest to where we think they are now."

"Working."

The holoimage of the yoga instructor returned.

"Cass?"

"I lean toward Janish's strategy. Divide and conquer. Lucinda, have we informed the targets about how to defeat the Megvesnaith?

"You mean have we told them to take off and nuke them from orbit. Yes, we told governing councils. It's the only way to be sure."

"Did you just paraphrase Aliens?"

"Yeah, but don't tell Nick."

The women laughed before Lucinda continued. "Bonnie?"

"Lucinda, I know what is going to happen."

"I knew your Nona. I trusted her Second Sight. I suspect you have it also. Would you care to enlighten us? Maybe a hint or two?"

"They all die."

"Who?"

"The Megvesnaith. They all die."

"When you say *all*, you mean the carriers?"

"Yes ... No ... Yes ... I mean ... All the Megvesnaith, all of them, are on the carriers. We destroy the carriers. We eliminate the

Megvesnaith."

None of the women had considered the results of their actions might be total genocide of an intelligent race. They sat in contemplative silence until Lucinda decided the session was over. Standing, rolling up her mat, she closed the discussion.

"We will discuss this with the crew, consider all options, but giving the bastards an option with an out will only allow them to delay and rebuild. No more plundering for slaves by the Megvesnaith."

Dugr, Galley

Lucinda has ordered an all-hands breakfast meeting to finalize their planning.

"Lucinda, the communications relay station in the remote sector we are monitoring has come online."

"Landry, are you sure?"

"Yes, the Megvesnaith are attempting to reach their carrier we designated Alpha."

"That means we know where they are and confirms they took the communications relay offline. If they are using the communications relay network, their technology must be compatible. Can we communicate with them?"

"Yes, they use an older version of the interstellar communications protocol."

Corb took over, leading the discussion. "We have reached the tipping point. Landry, give us your final tactical assessment."

"From their current location, they can arrive in each system simultaneously if Megvesnaith orders two carriers to Plentari. Two carriers to K'an and the Alpha carrier continues to Sol.

"Factoring in multiple entry points. The second carrier will enter Plentari two full cycles or about forty-four hours after the first invasion force arrives. Arrival estimates are approximately the same as the planet K'an.

"They are sacrificing Alpha to ensure one of the other two objectives does not fail.

"The summary is: The division of their fleet is the most likely scenario. Plentari or K'an, possibly both, will fall to the Megvesnaith."

Letting Landry's summary sink in, Corb continued. "Tipping point. We need to decide. Where do we go? Who do we help?"

Bonnie's voice is soft and subdued. "Wait, something is not right."

"Bonnie?"

"Dad, something is not right. I do not know what, but I can feel it."

"How can we help?"

"Wait ..."

Nona's, Kitchen

A week after her Nona's funeral, Bonnie, her mother Michelle, and her grandmother are seated at the kitchen table. When they see the faraway look, the thousand-mile stare, come over Bonnie, the older women sit quietly.

They do not see the imagery in Bonnie's head, but they accept her Second Sight reality.

Bonnie is standing on a deck, facing a portal. Stars are everywhere, the crest of a planet emerging from below.

With battle-scars and plasma laser burns streaking its hull, a large carrier floats over the planet disgorging fighters from its many portals. Hundreds of attack fighters are spewing out toward the planet. The massive ship opens a dozen hatches. Fueling nozzles extend from the hatches.

A dozen small tankers emerge from portals that expelled the fighters. Each tanker maneuvers and attaches to a fueling nozzle.

They are taking on the bioweapon.

The first tanker filled, it severs its connection to the nozzle. A small reddish-black ooze seeps from the tip of the nozzle. The remaining tankers emulate the process. A dozen small reddish-black amorphous blobs float in space and begin drifting toward the planet.

The fighters have formed their attack profile.

A dozen cone-shaped formations.

The small tankers maneuver to fill the open end of a cone created by the attack fighters.

When the twelve formations are aligned, as one, they begin their attack run on the planet.

The twelve-abreast formation begins swooping down, coming on-line, taking on the contour of the planet. Entering the atmosphere, fighter and tanker noses and their wings' tips start to glow with the heat.

The planetary defenses gush a shower of laser batteries. From stationary space platforms and ground installations, thousands of plasma laser beams illuminate the planet.

Attacking fighters are dropping by the dozens, but the attack formation does not break. The defensive cone formations continue to morph to protect the tankers. Like a flock of birds, the attack fighters morph and adapt when fighters fall out of alignment.

Entering the planet's Exosphere, the freighters each open a dozen belly ports. When the small tankers reach the planet's Mesosphere, injector booms appear, they begin infusing the weapon into the planet's atmosphere.

It is over.

The planet will become Megves Prime II.

Blinking, Bonnie is back in her Nona's kitchen. With respect for her passed-on mother, Bonnie's grandmother chooses to be called Nana.

Nana eases her granddaughter's concern.

"Your Nona used to do that. But not as intense. You must have learned something important."

"Yes, Nana, I think it is important, but I do not know why or how I can help."

"Not everything Nona saw came to pass. She often said what she saw was the future today. Tomorrow is a different future."

Dugr, Galley

"Landry put up images of Earth, K'an, Plentari, and Kripkeni."

At Bonnie's request, the monitors change to tiled images of the requested planets.

"That one. Kripkeni. That is the planet I saw in my Second Sight."

"Are you sure?"

"Yes, dad, I am sure. Kripkeni."

"What happened at Kripkeni?"

Bonnie hesitated before answering. When she spoke, her tone felt more Plentari than human. "We make a mistake. We defended the wrong planet. When we realized the error, the Triad reacted.

"The *Dugr* is fast, but we are not fast enough. We arrive, and it is too late. The attack has begun. The Megvesnaith sacrifice thousands to conquer the planet. They want the Garune people."

Uncharacteristically, Nick interrupts in a soft, pleasant tone. "Wait up, Little Bit. I believe you. The Garune are a warrior race. You have to fight just to talk to them. They don't kill too many anymore, but they are not afraid of battle. Are you sure?"

"Yes, Nick, I am sure. It is Kripkeni the Megvesniath want. They must have ignored the Garune battle challenge. They flew straight for the planet. The Garune were unable to stop at least one invasion carrier.

"Lucinda, everyone, it is the Garune they want, I am positive."

"We can assume two targets with certainty: Earth and Kripkeni. That leaves the third target. Maybe a fourth. Was it only one carrier you saw?"

"That is a good question. The carrier I saw was badly battle-scarred. I can't be sure, but I think it must have survived by sacrificing the second carrier.

"Also, I saw a lot more fighters from the one carrier than we saw in the Megves system. Either they moved the fighters to one carrier, or they have a lot more fighters than we counted."

"That will be our working assumption: Kripkeni and the Garune is the second target. The third target: Plentari or K'an?"

Hemming and hawing, everyone quietly deflected until JJ spoke.

"Captain, it is Plentari."

"Why, Plentari?"

"Slaves."

"Holy shit! He's right!"

"Yes, Cass, he is right. Plentari is eighty-eight percent female. The Megvesnaith need to repopulate. Landry, are the Megvesnaith and the Plentari biologically compatible."

"Working ...

"I am unable to find any reference to the Plentari and the Megvesnaith being biologically compatible ..."

"Wait!"

Everyone turned again to Cass. "Landry, check the index, look for the phrase 'seeded' or 'seeding' or 'genetic.'"

"Working ..."

"Cass, what index?"

Cass deferred Corey's question by turning to Lucinda. Lucinda looked up from frantically keying her small command console.

"Lieutenant Murphy, the index Cass referred to is on a need-to-know basis. It is highly classified. Knowing of its existence and discussing it with anyone will result in execution for treason. As captain of this vessel, I assure you I will not hesitate to perform a summary execution.

"Do you understand?"

"I understand. What index?"

"Good. Do not forget. Landry?"

Corb stepped on the response. "Landry, you

are to begin and maintain a scan of personal logs and correspondence. Encrypted or otherwise. If you find any reference to the index or anything else deemed classified, you will inform Lucinda. No information of any type is to be shared with anyone else. I mean no one.

"If you find a violation, you inform Lucinda and no one else. Understood?"

"Confirmed."

Lucinda was looking around, everyone returning the affirmative.

"Good. Landry, please continue."

"Cass was correct. The Plentari and the Megvesnaith are biologically compatible."

Corb continued. "Tipping point. We have to make some decisions and quickly. Lucinda, we need to update Michelle and Josh."

Lucinda stopped keying her command console before looking up and responding.

"Corb, we need to update everyone we think is a primary target. I have drafted a message. Landry, please put it on the monitors."

DEFENSE STRATEGY

MEGVESNAITH INVASION FORCE

CONFIRMATION UPDATE

DO NOT LET THE MEGVESNAITH IN-SYSTEM

DESTROY THE CARRIER AT EMERGENCE

Probable Targets

Earth: One Megvesnaith Invasion Carrier
Plentari: One/Two Megvesnaith Invasion Carrier(s)
Kripkeni: One/Two Megvesnaith Invasion Carrier(s)
K'an: One Megvesnaith Invasion Carrier

Confirmed: The Megvesnaith will attack using biological subjugation. The release of the biological subjugation agent will result in all life being eliminated or absorbed by the Megvesnaith.

Destroy the attacking carrier by disrupting its antimatter containment field.

No other options are viable.

**DO NOT LET THE MEGVESNAITH IN-SYSTEM
DESTROY THE CARRIER AT EMERGENCE**

"We send this to the governing bodies for each planet listed. For everyone else, we send the same message with the probable targets omitted. Let them continue to prepare their defenses."

Lucinda hesitated just enough for Beth to chime. "Do we provide an ETA for the attack?"

"Good point. I'll add the ETA. Landry?"

ETA TO EMERGENCE

Sol: One-Point-Seven Days
Plentari: Two-Point-Four Cycles
Kripkeni: Two-Point-One Cycles
K'an: One-Point-Nine Cycles

"Does that seem a little odd to anyone else?"

The crew turned to Corey, who continued his question.

"It seems a little too neat and tidy for me. Three, maybe four attacks simultaneously, across the galaxy, about two days from now. What are we missing?"

Cass was gentle in her response. "You forget the basic understanding of galactic history. All of these planets are in the Goldilocks Zone. These specific worlds are all capable of supporting life, including human life.

"It is not a coincidence all the races we encounter are biologically similar. Did the Academy not teach galactic history? Did they teach the history of the original Overlords?"

"They did, but I think you are talking about the Origin Theory. No one thinks the Origin Theory is valid. It is a convenient myth."

Cass was stupefied. Shaking her head side-to-side at the Lieutenant's comment, she looked to Corb for help.

"Corey, Bonnie, the Origin Story is not a myth, and it is legitimate. We have seen the source. The Divine intervention that began the

177

process of conscious life is unknown. We know, we have proof, the First manipulated sentient life in the galaxy.

"Beth?"

"Corey, what Corb is telling you is a fact. I have seen history. I was there. I know what happened with the Muh'xan.

"It is not a myth."

Corey persisted. "Why did they manipulate sentient life?"

Corb's cold response closed the topic.

"Because they could."

Part Four

Turn away from false destinies.

Plentari, Training Academy

"Counselor, the legends in the scrolls are confusing and hard to believe. The tales and legends are for children."

"The legend of Aalborinn and the Seekers of Blood, is it for children?"

"Counselor, on Earth, we have many fairy tales, stories for children, that are full of evil characters. Characters who eat children. But they are just stories. No one believes they are true."

"Is it true, many humans did not believe in little gray men until The Redeemer re-opened the star-portal to K'an?"

"Yes, that is true."

"There are many people across the galaxy, with fairy tales of little green men coming in the night to steal children. Might that also be true?"

Bonnie had no response. The Counselor continued.

"Aalborinn, you are attempting to refuse your destiny. When I gave you the assignment, you told me, 'I have seen a future. There is no assurance our actions today will not change the future.'

"I ask you again, are you ignoring your Second Sight?"

"No, Counselor."

"Good. Butterfly, what do you think of the fairy tale: Aalborinn and the Seekers of Blood?"

More Plentari than Human in her response, Bonnie's tone is firm and severe.

"I have seen the future. I understand my destiny. I will not look away from my responsibility."

Bonnie understood she had passed the test and pleased the Counselor.

Dugr, Galley

"Bonnie!"

"Sorry, Lucinda, I was thinking about a lesson from the academy. A lesson about the Plentari legends. Sorry, what is the question?"

"Do you think we are following the correct strategy?"

"I am not sure. I remembered something that may be important soon. Will you summarize the strategy for me?"

Lucinda controlled her exasperation.

"One, we let Admiral Turner defend Earth and Sol.

"Two, we insist the Madame Negotiator split her forces evenly, cover both emergence points, and follow Corb's strategy for defense.

"Three, we arrive at Kripkeni before the Megvesnaith. We destroy the carriers before they can attack the Garune. We will rely on the Garune delaying or killing one of the attacking carriers.

"Four, we let Commodore Jexond defend

K'an. If the Megvesnaith does not send two carriers to Kripkeni, we race back and help the Ajawlil defend K'an."

Bonnie continued with a subdued tone. "If the Megvesnaith do not consolidate their forces, one planet is going to be conquered. Planet K'an is the closest to Earth and has a permanent star-portal connection to Earth. Is the risk of letting K'an fall worth exposing Earth?"

The crew's silence told Bonnie she had asked the right question. Her response felt Plentari. Pressing on, she aligned the *Dugr's* crew to the future she knew to be real.

The bubbly girl everyone knew was gone.

"Letting K'an fall will expose Earth. We cannot let the Megvesnaith conquer K'an to subjugate the Ch'en. If they take K'an, they will then align with whoever agrees to assault and conquer Earth."

Lucinda vented but quickly suppressed her frustration. "Damn it. She's right. We are trying to wedge our desire to protect everyone into the facts. The facts have holes. To close the gaps, we need to make choices.

"Landry?"

"Yes, Captain?"

"I want percentages. Probability. Where are the Megvesnaith going to attack? Also, an assessment of the plausible success of the defense strategies."

"I anticipated the questions. Nothing is certain. Therefore, nothing in the analysis is one hundred percent.

"The threat to Earth approaches certainty. Defense success nears certainty. Admiral Turner will not let Earth fall to invaders.

"Plentari is the second-highest probability. The Megvesnaith will attack from two directions. The Plentari are probably already singing songs of courage for those standing to the line. Plentari will not fall.

"Kripkeni is the next highest probability. I used Bonnie's vision to align the analysis parameters. As you know, visions are not facts. It is fifty-fifty whether the Megvesnaith attack Kripkeni with two carriers or split the force and attack with one.

"The Kripkeni can defeat one attacking carrier, not two.

"If the Megvesnaith choose to divide their force, a second carrier will attack K'an and the Ch'en people.

"No other sentient systems are close enough to provide the anticipated simultaneous attack.

"If two carriers attack Kripkeni and the *Dugr* is in the system, Kripkeni will not fall.

"Any other scenario has either Kripkeni or K'an falling to the Megvesnaith."

"One more question. Can the *Death to All* defeat a Megvesnaith carrier before it makes it in-system?"

Landry had an unusually soft tone in his response. "Yes, Captain, it is possible for the *Death to All* to defeat a Megvesnaith carrier. The Ajawlil carrier can destroy the Megvesnaith invader using Corb's strategy.

"However, the battlecruiser *Death to All* will not survive the battle. The commodore could order the *Death to All* could rupture its antimatter containment field in the invading carrier's proximity. It is uncertain if Commodore Jexond is willing to fight a battle, he cannot survive."

Nick blurted. "We are right fucked."

The crew strained to hear Lucinda's melancholy voice. "Yes, Nick, this is a rough one."

In boxing terms, Nick rang the bell, calling the combatants to the ring. "Lucinda, pull up your big girl panties and tell us what we are going to do. Everyone here is behind you. We can't save everyone, but we can kick ass and take names.

"Whatever you decide, we got your back."

"Thanks, Nick. NT?"

"You know my feelings. Defend Earth first."

"Ragnar?"

"Defend Earth."

"I see a pattern developing. Anyone have another suggestion?"

"Yes."

Heads snapped around to Bonnie, but before she can speak, Lucinda issues an order.

"Alright, let's get up to the bridge and continue this discussion. I want to be underway in one hour."

Death to All, Bridge

The corpulent Commodore climbed into his command chair while issuing orders.

"Report."

"Commodore, we are in position, one-half lightyear from the emergence point. The fighter squadrons have been deployed and are patrolling the emergence point. There are no unaccounted-for vessels in the system."

"Very well. Inform the K'an Planetary Council of our arrival. Inquire about assistance."

"Assistance Commodore?"

"Yes, ask the Ch'en bastards if they are sending any help out here to stand with us."

"Understood."

Hákarl, Bridge

Built using the *Jaguar* as a template, the *Hákarl* is a smaller version of the *Dugr*. Josh feels at home on the bridge of his old ship.

"Admiral Turner, all ships report ready."

"Very well, Captain, issue the order."

The *Hákarl's* captain did not mind Admiral

Turner sitting in his command chair. The ship's newly appointed captain had not experienced real battle.

"Admiral, a question if I may?"

"Go ahead, Captain, but you may not like the answer."

"You know what I am going to ask?"

"I can guess, but ask anyway."

"Admiral, can we defeat the Megvesnaith?"

"Captain, you have seen the mission brief. You saw the video from the *Dugr*. One small attack ship destroyed a carrier. We have two Plentari Class carriers. Thirty-nine heavy cruisers. Sixteen lite freighters. Six-hundred, ninety-nine assorted fighters, cruisers, shuttles, and intra-stellar freighters. That adds up to seven hundred and fifty-six ships. Can we defeat the invaders? Captain, what do you think?"

"The *Dugr* is no *small attack* ship. I think a lot of people are going to die."

"That is defeatist thinking, not productive, and a detriment to morale on the eve of battle."

Looking around, Josh saw the crew was looking at their station's monitors, but their heads were turned or tilted to his conversation.

"I will indulge in your concern. It is a fact: People die in war. Tell me, Captain, do the lives of billions justify sacrificing the lives of hundreds or thousands?"

"Does the end justify the means? That

question ignores the moral and ethical uncertainty: Is it right?"

"Captain Miller, you are thinking like a human. From what we know of the other sentients, must humans change their collective ethos? What do you think is the correct response to an invasion force?"

The Captain realized he had argued himself into a corner. "Comms, report."

"Captain, all ships report underway. ETA to station keeping, fifty-six hours."

"Very well, point-four *c*, let's get there."

"Captain Miller?"

"Yes, Admiral?"

"Jump us to the position."

"Admiral, regulations do not permit using the star-portal within the solar system."

"Captain, I am aware of the regulations. I wrote most of the protocols. I am sorry, I was unclear. Captain Miller, you are ordered to use the *Hákarl's* star-portal to position us at the outer marker."

"Yes, Admiral. Navigation, plot the jump."

"Aye, Captain."

Josh noticed the bridge crew one-by-one waited for the Captain's back to being turned away so they could give a thumbs up or a nod of approval.

Plentari, Main Hall

"Madame Negotiator, the message is authentic."

The Plentari leader turned away from the messenger toward her loyal friend. "We will not let the Plentari become slaves and breeding stock for those whose lips drip with blood.

"Commander Jirxena, see to the defense."

"Yes, Madame Negotiator."

Death to All, Bridge

"Commodore, we have received a response from the Ch'en Council."

The commodore's stubby fingers pressed the icons on his command chair's console. Reading the message twice, he understood the truth of the mission. Grunts of disgust from the commodore resulted in the XO's inquiry.

"Sir, is there a problem?"

"The Redeemer knew this was going to happen. The Ch'en have no defense capability. They expect us to stop the invasion. They have conspired with the Megvesnaith."

"Commodore?"

"This line from the message: 'We are confident you will be victorious in destroying the approaching vessel.' The Ch'en bastards know something about the approaching force."

Dugr, Bridge

"Bonnie, you keep eluding to something, you know. Maybe if you share your thoughts and knowledge, it will help us understand and guide our decision on what we need to do next."

"Lucinda, we need to protect Earth. What I do not understand is why the Megvesnaith will split their force. There is something ... A story. Plentari legends and lore possess a level of reality. A Plentari legend I read at the academy keeps coming back to me."

"Aalborinn and the Seekers of Blood?"

"No, JJ, not that one. The story about the hidden truth. I think it was titled ... I forget its title. It does not matter. The story is similar to the Earth legend of the Trojan Horse."

"Maldorin and the Secret Box."

"Yes, Maldorin and the Secret Box. Two warring people want to make peace. Maldorin gives Fortunic, the enemy, a puzzle box that is said to contain the path to peace. But the box does not hold a secret. The secret is the box is a diversion. While Fortunic is distracted trying to open the box, Maldorin steals the souls of Fortunic's family."

JJ was impressed. "That is the legend. Do you think it applies to us?"

"Yes, I do. The question is, which carrier is the secret box? Cass, from what we know, which of the target planets has the least value to the

Megvesnaith?"

"Good question. Landry?"

"Cass, to answer the question, we need to know the priorities of the Megvesnaith."

"YES!"

The outburst caused everyone to turn toward Beth, who had surprised herself at the sharpness of her comment. Nick was not going to let it pass. "Bloody 'ell, my ears!"

"Suck it up, Uncle Nick. Lucinda, I think I know what they are doing. One carrier headed to Earth and the one headed to K'an are the secret boxes. They are diversions designed to pull Corb from the real targets."

"Holy shit!"

Lucinda verbally ribbed her friend. "Cass, I liked it better when you didn't swear. Beth, I think you are right. Corb?"

Corb deflected. "Bonnie?"

"Me?"

"Yes, you ... Forget it. I'll ask JJ."

"Redeemer?"

"JJ, the legend of Aalborinn and the Seekers of Blood. Jump to the end, what happens?"

"Redeemer, I do not understand."

"Yes, you do and stop being coy. You are here for a reason. Now tell me what I want to know."

Corb's tone forced Bonnie to intercede and defend her friend. "JJ will tell you, but there is no need to make him do something that makes him uncomfortable. I will tell you what you want to know.

"First, I have a question."

Corb's gemstone blue eyes were sparkling, his bright smile a radiant reminder of his heart. "It is about time."

Bonnie ignored the barb. "It is two questions. First, do you trust the Ajawlil to do what is necessary to defend K'an?"

"I do not."

"I suspected as much. Second question, are you prepared to destroy K'an to destroy the Megvesnaith if they gain control of K'an and the Ch'en people?"

Outwardly, Corb remained unchanged. His mind was reeling, but he answered. "Humans are living on K'an ... We cannot allow the Megvesnaith to control K'an."

Turning to Lucinda, Bonnie decided for the crew of the *Dugr*. "We send a message to the Ajawlil Commodore. Then we must arrive at Kripkeni before the Megvesnaith."

"Why?"

"Because, if I am going to fulfill the legend, we need to go to Kripkeni."

Everyone except JJ was considering the phrase " ... if I am going to fulfill the legend ... " With uncharacteristic animation for a Plentari, JJ's response was firm. "You are Aalborinn, Daughter of the Redeemer, First Daughter of the Plentari."

"Yes, JJ. But I am also Bonnie, daughter of Michelle, and I will do something my Nona told me about before she passed. She said ... it does not matter what she said. We can change our actions today, which will change tomorrow."

"The Butterfly Effect."

"Yes, Nick, the Butterfly Effect. But..."

"It is a false, circular argument."

"Yes, Cass, it is. So, what is different? Why was I given one image only to be here now, attempting to alter our path?"

It was JJ who filled the gap. "Because Aalborinn, you were given a vision of what is possible if you do not act correctly."

"How is that possible?"

"Aalborinn, you ask questions that do not have answers. How is it possible for your mind to see that which has not occurred?"

"I do not know."

JJ continued in the formal conversational tone typical to the Plentari. Individual titles are an intentional reminder of the person's stature and position. "Aalborinn, for the Plentari, you were given Sight to see the history of the future and the alternative ..."

"Go on."

"Aalborinn, you must do that which is required."

Bonnie chose a long pause in which she

refused to look anywhere but at her father before responding. Remembering the sessions with the counselor, she replied timidly. "I will not look away from my responsibility."

Lucinda closed the discussion. "You two will tell us about this legend, but right now, we are going to blow this pop stand. The question is, where are we going? Bonnie, this seems to come down to you. Where do we go?"

"Beth is correct. The Megvesnaith want two things to survive. They want the Plentari as slaves, and they want the shipbuilding docks and repair depot at Kripkeni.

"Breeding the slaves will rebuild their population. Access to ships, and shipbuilding, will let them resume plundering the galaxy.

"Let Uncle Josh destroy the invaders at Sol. Jirxena will defend Plentari with her life. We will help the Garune defend Kripkeni."

"K'an?"

"Lucinda, if K'an falls ... If we are wrong ... If the invasion carrier Alpha is marching on Sol, and the carrier they send to K'an are not diversions. If they are not secret boxes, then we live with the consequences. Dad?"

"Yes, Bonnie?"

"Send a message to the Commodore. Tell him he stops the Megvesnaith from entering the K'an system, or you will destroy the Ajawlil factories on Zerain.

"If the Commodore does not stop the invasion, we will terminate the Ajawlil. If you are not willing ... I am."

Corb did not debate the request. "Landry, send the message from me. You know which one."

"Sending."

"You prepared for this?"

"Yes, I thought it might boil down to blackmail. It is not the first time for our merry band of miscreants."

"Lucinda, we need to beat the Megvesnaith to Kripkeni. Can we do it?"

"Aalborinn, we are going to try, like hell. Rotating shifts starting now. Second shift report in eight hours. Nick, get us going. Entry at point-eight-one *c*. We are going to re-write the quantum calculations. Landry, check his work."

Nick's tone, a soft inquiry. "Lucinda, point-eight-one *c*, are you sure?"

"Yes, Nick. We are going to see how fast we can fly. Beth, I want around-the-clock, eyes-on monitoring of the *Dugr*. Landry, check Nick's calculations and help Beth monitor the *Dugr*. Put some of that excess capacity you claim to have to use."

"Checking."

Death to All, Bridge

"Commodore, we have received a message

from The Redeemer."

"Captain, you mean a message from the *Dugr*?"

"No, Commodore, the message is from The Redeemer."

"Decrypt it and forward it to my console."

"Commodore, the message is not encrypted."

The Commodore looked down, pressed the icon, and read the short message. When he looked up, the entire bridge crew was staring at him.

"No one lives forever."

"Commodore, you cannot possibly consider these actions."

"Captain, I was dealing with The Redeemer before your slime became solid, and you slipped out of the birth canister. There is one thing I know about The Redeemer. He never fails to fulfill his promises."

"Commodore, what promise?"

"You read the message, Captain. You tell me."

The Captain read, then re-read the message, before he understood.

"The Redeemer knows the K'an and the Xjaal have conspired with the Megvesnaith."

"Excellent, Captain. Now that you understand, why do you think the Redeemer has issued the order?"

"Commodore, I do not know."

"I will let you think about it. I am revising the battleplan. We will review the new plan in an hour."

Hákarl, Bridge

"Admiral, we are in position, station-keeping at the outer-marker. No activity reported at the emergence point."

"Thank you, Captain."

"There is a new message from Mister Johnson, addressed to you."

"You mean a message from the *Dugr*?"

"No, Admiral, the message is classified as personal and is from Mister Johnson. It is addressed to you."

"Very well."

Josh pressed the correct icons and read the message before looking around the bridge at the young faces. Pressing a few more icons, he issued the orders.

"Captain transmit the new defense strategy to the fleet. The fleet is to position as described in the new plan."

The captain relayed the orders while reading the new defense plan. "Comms, issue the Admiral's orders to the fleet."

"Sending now."

"Admiral, is this correct?"

"Captain, I am a tolerant person by nature,

but I am not appreciative of you second-guessing my orders. I will not ask this again. Are you capable of following my orders?"

"Admiral, with respect..."

"Captain, you are relieved. Security escort Captain Miller to his cabin. Commander Weaver, you are now the Captain of this boat. Any questions?"

"One question, Admiral."

"Go ahead, Comman ... Captain."

"Will they sing songs about us?"

"Yes, they will sing songs about us. Comms, connect me to the fleet."

Several tones indicate the communications channel opening. The communications officer turned to the admiral and nodded.

"This is Admiral Turner. Today is the day we find out if Humans are ready to step up and defend their homeworld. Defend Earth without help from across the galaxy.

"Your Captains have just received the revised defense plan. We are going to defend Earth by attacking. The best defense is a good offense.

"The plan is solid. We have used it before. I know the fleet is ready. I am making a small adjustment to the attack plan. Instead of one long CLJ maneuver, we will create a series of CLJ attack profiles. What I want to know is, where are the volunteers to lead each profile?

"We stand together, or Earth will fall to

slavers. The Megvesnaith invasion force will not enter our home. Admiral Turner out."

"Admiral, volunteers are flooding the comms channels."

"Send a message. Here's what I want to happen."

Dugr, Bridge

The riser's symbols were overwhelmingly bright and hot enough to create physical pain for anyone too close. Only Beth monitoring the ship, and Lucinda, who was on Triad rotation, remained on the bridge.

"Landry, we have been in the slipstream for hours, flying faster than we thought possible. We must be close to Kripkeni. Should we drop into normal space and use a star fix to plot our location? If we drop into standard space, you can calculate our true velocity."

"Beth, the calculations are being written and re-written. If we drop out early, we may not make the Kripkeni system before the Megvesnaith."

Before Beth can respond, the bridge doors slid open.

"Bonnie?"

Bonnie spoke without acknowledging Beth. "Lucinda, you can drop out of the slipstream. Landry, call up the crew."

With a nod from Beth to Landry's avatar, the

Dugr reacts to reentering standard space. Pulling off her protective goggles, Beth is talking to Landry but looking at Bonnie.

"Landry report."

"I can ping a Kripkeni outer marker. We were going to overshoot Kripkeni. Miss Wilbon was correct to drop into normal space."

The crew begins arriving on the bridge. Beth continues with a nod from Lucinda. "Bonnie, how did you know?"

"I felt the connections. I sensed we were close."

"Felt? Connections? How? We were in the other reality, not in standard space."

"You know we can see the connections in our mind's eye. It is one of the powers which allows us to bond to people across space."

"I understand. You think your ability to see the points of light, the connections, is related to your ability to control the trilateral domain. I need more. How did you *feel* standard space and know it was time to drop out of the slipstream?"

"I am not sure, but I think it is ... We never really leave normal space. It is named *the trilateral domain* because it has three parts. Dark Matter. Dark Energy. The third is normal space."

Lucinda resumed command. "Nick?"

"We are half a lightyear from the outer marker. We are point-seven lightyears from the primary hyper-tunnel emergence point. Two-point two lightyears from the other emergence point."

"Plot jumps to both emergence points. Be ready. Landry, contact Kripkeni control, tell them we are here, ask for a meeting with the Supreme War Committee.

"Beth?"

"The ship is fine, Lucinda. I think its design is purpose-built to fly that fast. Probably faster."

"Ragnar, I want a firing solution for both emergence points. When we know what the Kripkeni have planned, we will adjust."

"Roger that."

"Landry?"

"Yes, Captain?"

Lucinda is feeling the pressure. Minor annoyances are creating internal angst. She senses this may be the end of her crew.

"Don't be coy. I do not like the new Landry. I don't like Cass swearing. Landry being evasive and passive grates on me. I don't like it. Landry, what have you learned?"

"The Kripkeni have mustered their forces at the primary emergence point. They did not split their battle groups to cover both emergence points."

"Do you know why they chose to defend one and not both?"

"I do not. We can speculate the Supreme War Committee issued a directive."

"When do we expect the first invasion carrier

to arrive?"

"Between sixteen and twenty-six hours."

Death to All, Bridge

"Commodore, the Ch'en Council is requesting a meeting."

The Commodore's new uniform stretched taut around his body. Resplendent in purple and gold, the crew is singing songs about victories.

"Captain. Why do you think the Redeemer has issued the order?"

"Commodore, the invaders are a diversion."

"Correct."

"What if we are wrong. What if the invaders are not a diversion?"

"Captain, what does it matter? We must destroy the invaders and any possibility of exposure to the weapon.

"Put the Ch'en scum on the main monitor."

The Ch'en Planetary Executive Council appears. The equivalent of a Prime Minister is seated in the middle of a trio. Large head, grayish-blue skin tone, three fingers on elongated arms, outwardly, the Ch'en are gender-neutral. The Prime Minister is known to be female.

"How may I help you?"

"Commodore, we are inquiring about your battle plans. We did not receive a reply to our inquiry and became concerned. Do you have a plan to defeat the Megvesnaith, who will arrive soon to attack our peaceful home?"

"Do I have a plan? Yes, I plan to depart K'an and return to my home in one hour."

"Commodore, you cannot be serious. Our defenses are not capable of preventing the invasion."

"I am serious. Tell me, Chancellor, or Chairperson, or whatever you call yourself, why did it take you so long to contact me directly?"

"I do not understand. When you did not reply to our inquiry, we requested this meeting."

"What you mean is you became worried when I did not confirm our willingness to die for you. You are cowards."

"Insults are not required. Insults disrupt the Harmony."

"I will tell you what will disrupt the Harmony. When the Megvesnaith begin spraying your planet with their weapon, that will disrupt the harmony."

"Commodore, that is unlikely. We understand ... We acquired information. The Redeemer has ordered you to defend K'an."

Scoffing and waving a derisive dismissal, the commodore continued.

"You think it is unlikely the invaders will attack K'an. That is interesting. You are of the misconception because of our loyalty to The Redeemer. Do you believe we will gladly give up our lives to save another species? A species that has spent millennia manipulating and scheming to secure their *harmony*.

"I think you will have a lot of fun with your new overlords."

Turning from the monitors, the Commodore issued new orders. "Captain, we depart in one hour."

The Chancellor persisted. "Commodore, please, we have little …"

Interrupting, the Commodore calls her bluff. "Tell me, Chancellor, why is it you are concerned? Is it possible, when we leave, your deal with the Xjaal and the Megvesnaith will dissolve? Do you not trust your new partners?"

"Commodore, please stand by." On the monitor, the Chancellor's long finger pressed a short series of icons. The conference was muted. The three Ch'en leaders began an animated debate.

"Comms cut the link."

Ship's monitors reverted to space and the location of the hyper-tunnel emergence point.

"Commodore, the Ch'en council is requesting the meeting resume."

"Do not respond. Let the bastards wait. Stand down the order to depart. I will meet with the squadron commanders."

Hákarl, **Bridge**

Josh and the *Hákarl's* chief pilot, Captain Mari Claire Patterson, are talking and joking. Both officers in the United States Air Force were temporarily assigned to the TC3 space command. They consider the fraternal bond an advantage.

"Admiral, is it true about the name, the *Hákarl?*"

"Is what true?"

"The name, does it mean Shark?"

"Yes, that is accurate. Right now, though, I am interested in how Eric Clapton got the nickname 'Slowhand.' Do you know how he got the nickname?"

"No, sir."

"According to his biography, he used light-gauge guitar strings, a skinny first string, which made it easier to bend the notes. His frenetic bits of playing broke a lot of strings. While he was changing a string on stage, the British audiences would start a slow handclap. That inspired a friend, someone from the band, I think, to call him 'Slowhand.' It is a good nickname. 'Slowhand' is short for slow handclap."

"That is a good story, but I don't understand."

"You are the pilot. You control where we are at any given moment. On stage, working with the drummer, the lead guitar player controls the music. If I am correct, Captain, about what we will need, I will be the drummer. We are going to need your fingers to be Eric Clapton fast. I want you to bend those icons like a bluesman bends his guitar strings."

"I think I understand. Admiral, what if I break a string?"

Looking at Captain Patterson's striking green eyes, Josh is considering their age difference. Ignoring his thoughts, he reminds the captain of her duty. "You break a string, Captain, we will eat an antimatter explosion."

Dugr, Bridge

With the Garune defenses arrayed at the primary hyper-tunnel emergence point, Lucinda had ordered the *Dugr* to a defensive position at the secondary emergence portal.

"Corb, I can't argue their point."

"I agree, Lucinda. The Garune Supreme War Committee assessment is accurate."

"Landry, assess the probability of the Garune fleet stopping a Megvesnaith carrier."

"Based on the number of vessels in their defensive alignment, if they use the CLJ maneuver, the probability scenarios, for success, average eighty-six percent. Assuming, of course, no significant changes to external variables."

"External variables?"

"Cass, the scenarios assume a predictive

pattern based on past actions. If the Megvesnaith change their pattern, the assessments range from unlikely to invalid."

Lucinda raised her 'what did you expect' eyebrows toward Cass before speaking. "The question is, how long do we wait for the second carrier before we jump over and help the Garune fleet with the first invader?"

"Captain, I have an idea."

"Go ahead, Landry."

"I can open a communications micro-wormhole from here to Q'eqchi. We can bounce off the outer markers to augment the signal. The connection at Q'eqchi will re-direct to Jol on the space station. Jol can connect to K'an on the permanent link.

"We can monitor the Ch'en communications."

"Interesting. What makes you think the Ch'en Executive Council will grant permission for us to monitor their communications?"

"We are not going to ask for their permission."

"Damn. Landry, did you just suggest we spy on the Ch'en?"

"Yes, Captain."

"Maybe I do like the new Landry. You are growing on me. Will it be real-time communications?

"No, but it will be near real-time."

"Do it."

Cass remained unconvinced. "What will we learn? Also, can we talk to Josh?"

"With the comms link, we will know where the second carrier is as soon as it emerges. Landry, can Jol connect us to Josh?"

"Yes."

"Do it. Let me know when it is ready. Bonnie, I think it is storytime."

Bonnie waits for everyone to stop reading their console and focus on her.

"At the academy, I was required to read many of the Plentari stories and legends. It was mandatory for me to thoroughly understand the story titled: Aalborinn and the Seekers of Blood.

"The Plentari have a council of elders they call the Saga. On Earth, they are Priests, or Shaman, or Elders. To the Plentari, they are all those and more. Calling them Saga is correct. They are the keepers of the Plentari legends and tales. The Saga embody the history of the Plentari.

"For the Plentari, the Saga keep the stories alive. They do not consider their legends and tales are a form of history. They are stories of what will be the past or an account of history not yet written. The stories and lore are not fairy tales. At least not as we think of the term. Every fable or story is considered truth. Either it happened, is happening, or will happen.

"There is no concept of myth in the Plentari

culture.

"The Plentari view their stories and legends as history or a future to be written. Including the legend of Aalborinn and the Seekers of Blood.

"I was given the title, Aalborinn, Daughter of the Redeemer, First Daughter of the Plentari because, somehow, the Saga determined I am the Aalborinn of the legend.

"Aalborinn was a title before it was a name. It means 'Of Noble Birth' or 'Nobility Born.'

"For the Saga, it was a no-lose gamble conferring the title on a human. If I failed the academy, they would find a Plentari to fulfill the legend.

"The legend is not long. It is not even a short story. It is not a fable. It is concise, and every line has a deep meaning.

Aalborinn and the Seekers of Blood

Under the stars, she will stand to face her destiny.
From friends at her back, she will draw strength.
She weeps for the dead and rejoices at life.
Mercy is her pain.

Under the stars, hers is a destiny to create.
For death, she will be known.
Weeping and rejoicing, she is of two souls.
Mercy and pain are her companions.

Under the stars, she will not look away.

She does not turn away from her destiny.

It was JJ who broke the calm with an attempt to gently correct Bonnie on one small point.

"Aalborinn?"

"No, JJ."

More human than Plentari in his response, Bonnie knows he is challenging her to be truthful.

"Did you attend the academy? Are you Plentari?"

JJ had confronted Bonnie's Plentari pride. No Plentari, especially a Plentari Warrior, would hold back from the truth. Humbled, Bonnie corrects herself by repeating the last stanza accurately.

Under the stars, she will not look away.

From above, she rains death.

Weeping for the death, her friends rejoice.

Mercy is naught.

She does not turn away from her destiny.

Eventually, Cass breaks the painful stillness. "That is a lot to unpack. I read along while you recited the story. Every word was correct."

"I have read the story hundreds of times."

His voice weak and quivering, guessing it foretells of a dire future for Bonnie, Corey mumbles.

"Help me understand. What does it mean?"

Bonnie stares at the small man, letting Cass respond. "It means Aalborinn must act to save billions of lives. To save Earth, she must believe in herself. She must do that which is necessary even if it means sacrificing her life and the life of friends at her back. She will not look away."

"Friends at her back? I get it. That is us. Weeping for the death, her friends rejoice. What does that mean?"

"Yes, friends at her back is us. It is also the Plentari. It is Admiral Turner and the fleet defending Earth. Weeping for the death, her friends rejoice, means we, all of us, stand in support of Aalborinn, no matter the consequences."

Nick and Ragnar both leaned forward and tried to speak. Nick sat back and nodded to Ragnar. With a tone that indicated there was no debate, he told Corey what he needed to hear.

"We consider every mission before we sign-on. We understand every operation is a one-way quest before we sign the orders. To think otherwise is to deny reality. Every time we emerge into standard space, we might have to fight.

"There was a time before you were born when every hyper-tunnel emergence was an ambush. We fought and killed thousands.

"This is no different. I don't know what you think you signed up for or what you thought would happen on this mission. What I know is a simple truth. This is not a pleasure cruise.

"We are trying to prevent genocide. We will stop the enslavement of millions or billions.

"That means if we have to die helping each other, to save Earth, that is what we will do.

"If you did not sign up for that, too damn bad. This is where we are, and you are here with us. If Bonnie ... If Aalborinn needs us to stand at her back to protect Earth, that is what we are going to do."

Everyone remained still and silent until Cass stepped over to her husband and sat in Ragnar's lap. Janish stepped over to Nick and did the same. NT stood next to Lucinda's command chair, his hand on her shoulder. Everyone looked at everyone else until Bonnie broke the melancholy.

With her father's bright eyes, his radiant smile, and her mother's beauty, her presence filled the vacuum of space.

"My Nona used to tell me something interesting. She always said we control our destiny. She said: 'What I see in the Sight is the future today. Tomorrow is a different future.'

"I think the legends are one possible future. History is yet to be written. If history is yet to be written, why can't we be the author?"

"Bloody well right. If we are the author, we can change the plot."

"Exactly Nick. Sorry, Uncle Nick."

"Little Bit, call me Nick. You're too old for a child's tripe. Besides, Beth gets offended because I like you better."

Chuckling, Beth gave as good as she got. "Piss off, old sod."

Nick closed the topic. "Aalborinn, the Davies family has your back. We *all* have your back, even wiggle dick there."

Corey meekly nodded in agreement.

***Death to All*, Bridge**

"Commodore, the portal is opening."

"Alert the fighter groups."

"They are aware of the portal opening and are moving to intercept. Shall we power up the cannons?"

"Yes, Captain. Get Commander Jumury on the line."

"The line to Commander Jumury is open, Commodore."

"Commander Jumury, is your fleet ready?"

"Yes, Commodore. Today is a good day to die."

"Commander Jumury, you watch too many human cinemas. Good hunting, Commander."

The bridge crew watched the big Megvesnaith carrier emerge into standard space.

"What is it doing?"

"Commodore, it is rolling."

"Rolling?"

"Yes, Commodore, rolling. It is protecting its antimatter containment field. The constant roll means we cannot get a lock on the correct target location.

"Commander Jumury is requesting orders."

"A lathe."

The entire bridge crew turned to the security officer standing on-guard.

"Consider the vessel as a log turning on a lathe. As it spins, apply the cutter."

The Commodore pointed his finger at the security guard then at the communications officer. "Open a channel."

"This is Commodore Jexond. The invaders will not be able to launch their attack fighters while the invasion carrier is rolling. New orders: All attack fighters fire on the hull at a distance of ten kilometers. New firing coordinates are on their way.

"Gunner, I want the target to be a ring around the carrier's hull. Just forward of the engine pods. We will let the rolling movement cut the vessel in half."

"Targeting profile sent."

"Thank you, Gunner."

"Commodore, at ten kilometers, no fighters will survive the explosion."

"I am aware, Commander."

Hákarl, Bridge

"Admiral, we are picking up a spike in the alpha and gamma emissions from the emergence point."

"Thank you. Here we go, people. Comms, alert the fleet."

"Battle stations. Aye."

The klaxons begin wailing. Admiral Turner screamed over the noise. "Turn those damned things off."

The klaxons stopped, but the subdued, red-hued lighting remained.

"What the hell?"

"Admiral, the invasion ship is rolling. The rotational speed is one revolution per minute. At that rate, we will be unable to penetrate the hull sufficiently."

"Thank you, XO. Ideas?"

"We can blow holes in their hull. The atmo venting will slow the roll."

"No can do. We cannot allow the weapon to be released."

"Anyone else?"

Mari turned around and looked up to the Admiral. "Their mass is too great to stop the roll quickly. We know we have to rupture their antimatter to ensure the destruction of the invasion weapon.

"Instead of targeting one location. We target

the hull along a directrix forward of the engine nacelles."

Unblinking, Josh was looking at the pilot.

"The directrix? It is a transverse line that follows a point around a cylinder."

"You want to keep hitting the hull, along a single line, until we cut it in half, and they lose antimatter containment."

"Yes. Modify the CLJ maneuver. Instead of attacking a single point on the hull. Attack the directrix."

"Captain, that is brilliant. We will instruct the pilots to target the hull below three o'clock. Lay it out. Weapons?"

"Understood, Admiral. Plotting targeting now."

"Also, Admiral?"

"Yes, Captain Patterson."

"They are rotating too fast to be able to launch fighters."

"Excellent ... Weapons move our fighters in. Move up the fighters, get them close. I want every fighter to unload on that bastard right now. I want lasers and plasma torpedoes on that hull in thirty seconds."

The bridge crew's fingers were flying over consoles. Each person is speaking to someone, somewhere, moving fighters and lite carriers into position.

The forward monitors showed the fighters

merging into a line. One hundred and twenty-eight attack fighters lined up nose-to-tail for over five hundred kilometers. A microscopic distance in space terms but impressive. A second line of one hundred and twenty-eight attack fighters are forming further out, waiting for the approach run.

"Comms, give me ... Give me whoever is on point in that line."

"Captain Reynolds on the line, Admiral."

"Captain Reynolds, Admiral Turner here, didn't anyone ever tell you never to volunteer?"

"Yeah, Admiral, my momma always said I was none too bright."

"Captain Reynolds, they are all going to follow you. Can you do it?"

"Admiral, are you asking me if I can fly this thing up a gnat's ass and come out the other side smelling like roses?"

"Yes, Captain, that is what I am asking you."

"Admiral, we're living in high cotton."

"Good luck, Captain. Fly true. *Hákarl* out. Commander, if Captain Reynolds makes it back, he's a Major the moment his boots touch the deck."

"You can try, Admiral. Jessie Reynolds has turned down a promotion at least three times. He flies. He is a fighter pilot's fighter pilot."

"Understood.

"Comms, I want long-range images on the rat bastard ship."

The monitors morphed to a closer image.

"Navigation, are we far enough out to absorb the explosion?"

"No, sir, we are two-hundred and twenty-five thousand kilometers inside the projected safe zone boundary."

Captain Patterson looked over her shoulder. Josh nodded to the unasked question.

"Confirmed, new coordinates, one-seven-five, by two-two-four, by nine-three."

The crew felt the engines begin to push the *Hákarl* forward. His fingers flashing over his console, the ship's new captain turned to Josh, ashen and eyes wide.

"You are taking us closer?"

"Yes, XO, that is what I am doing."

"Admiral, I must protest."

"Noted."

"Arrival in ninety-seven seconds."

"Thank you, Captain Patterson."

"Admiral, I must object to this plan. You are putting the TC3's most valuable asset at unnecessary risk."

"Wrong. The TC3's most valuable asset is on the *Dugr*, fighting a similar battle."

"Admiral ..."

"XO, if you keep whining, I will have you removed."

"I will file a formal protest."

"You do that. File your resignation along with the protest. Sergeant, get him off my bridge.

Someone, find me a new XO."

The security sergeant steps forward before turning and following the demoted XO off the bridge.

"Admiral?"

"Yes, Lieutenant?"

"We have an incoming message from, hold while I confirm. It is from the *Dugr*. Audio only."

"Well, hell, what did they do now? Put it on my console."

Plentari, Main Hall

Large monitors are showing the global broadcast of the battle. Hundreds of Plentari fighters are buzzing around the invading carrier. Wave after wave of attack fighters are aligning to make a run on the invasion carrier from starboard.

The crew is targeting forward of the engine cowling. Enormous chunks of the composite hull are being cut away with every fighter's strafe.

The carrier's launch bays begin to open but retract when the invasion carrier begins a gentle roll.

The Plentari anticipate the roll defense and reconfigure their battery to approach from opposite the roll. Attack fighters buzzing like flies, their plasma cannons are creating superficial damage.

The first of the Saga breaks the silence.

"It is exactly as The Redeemer foretold."

The Madame Negotiator ignores the Saga. "Admiral, the damage is not sufficient to complete the objective."

"The battle is not complete."

Pressing a short series of icons on her tablet, the Admiral sealed the invading carrier's fate.

The Plentari fighters break off and regroup. Forming a line, they begin accelerating toward the slowly rolling carrier.

"Madame Negotiator?"

"Saga, the humans refer to it as the CLJ maneuver. Did you know Saga, The Redeemer's name as a child, was Corb Levi Johnson? Yes, of course, you did. What you see is our brave warriors executing the attack The Redeemer used to save his homeworld from the rogue Ajawlil Admiral."

"Yes, I know the story. Thank you for reminding me. The Redeemer was able to teleport out before impact."

"Yes, Saga, that is a truth."

"There are none braver than the Plentari."

"That is also a truth."

"Madame Negotiator, if they are successful, how many will survive?"

"Saga, they will be successful. None of our brave warriors will survive."

Dugr, **Bridge**

"Landry, say that again."

"The *Death to All* has engaged a Megvesnaith carrier in the K'an system."

"We can't sit here and do nothing. Nick, get us over to the primary emergence point. We are about to have company."

Nick pressed the familiar sequence of icons. The *Dugr* jumped to the Kripkeni main emergence point. The monitors adjusted to an image just outside the Garune defensive ring of fighters.

"Report."

"It is the carrier we classified as Echo. The Garune are beginning their attack runs using their normal attack profile. They are damaging the carrier's hull, but the damage is ineffective in creating the antimatter containment rupture."

"Damn. Okay. Nick, Ragnar, you're up. Weapons free, Landry, tell the Garune to run."

The monitors filled with Garune attack fighters. All turning, heading in-system.

"Nick, she's beginning to roll."

"Thank you, Landry. Help me with the adjustment. Ragnar, what do you think, one, two, or three runs?"

"Three? Do you think it will take me three runs to stop them? Just put me on target one-time, you limey twat."

Nick was laughing while he pressed icons. The *Dugr* re-appeared ten-thousand kilometers to the eleven o'clock of the carrier. The slow clockwise roll brought the target directly under the *Dugr's* weapons.

Ragnar did not countdown or announce weapons-free. The railguns screamed with six, three-ton bolts followed by the beams from the four plasma cannons lighting up the carrier. The plasma lasers arrived first, softening the hull.

Nick slid the *Dugr* on the z-axis, maintaining targeting alignment to the rotation of the carrier.

Beth issued a report. "They are opening their launch bays."

"Landry, can they launch while they are rolling?

"Captain, it appears as if they are going to try."

The second volley of the rail gun bolts screamed from the *Dugr*. The plasma cannons arriving before the heavy metal bolts. Lucinda did not like the way the battle was unfolding.

"Ragnar?"

"We hit them. The bolts penetrated the hull."

"Damage report, Landry?"

"Unknown. Recommend another round."

"Nick?"

"I'll get us out."

"Ragnar, do not miss. What is it, Beth?"

"Captain, we have company."

"JJ, you have the defense cannons."

"Stand by."

"What now, Beth?"

"Captain, Garune fighters are engaging the Megvesnaith. Fighters? Landry, explain."

"There are Garune attack fighters deliberately ramming the invading carrier. They are opening the hull at the target coordinates. It appears the Megvesnaith reinforced the target area."

"Ragnar?"

"Firing."

The crew watched the lasers strike the new crater in the carrier's hull. They were followed by the rail gun bolts, which also disappear into Carrier Echo's interior.

"NICK!"

Before Lucinda's scream faded, the *Dugr* was two lightyears above the Kripkeni elliptical plane. The invading carrier's antimatter containment ruptured. The explosion reached far enough to catch the end of the retreating Garune fighters.

Landry's tone was even. "Captain, we have a problem."

"What now?"

"There is a second Megvesnaith carrier in-system."

"What? Where the hell is it?"

The monitors change to a long-range image of the Kripkeni system.

"They came in behind us, from the other side

of the Kripkeni star.

"Is that one of the carrier's we saw at Megves Major?"

"No, this is a new ship, designated Golf."

"Landry, how big is that thing?"

"Lucinda, it is almost twice the tonnage of the other carriers we observed."

It was Bonnie who stated the obvious.

"We assumed they only had six carriers. This is the seventh. There might be more."

"Landry, you have one job right now. You break their comms. I want to know how many of these bastards are out there."

"Working."

"Options. Corb first?"

"I want to hear everyone else before I speak."

"Ragnar?"

"Carrier Golf has already deployed its fighters. We can't take them all, even with the Garune's help. By the time they get back, the Garune fighters will be low on fuel."

"Nick?"

"Captain, I got nothing. Tell me where to point us, and I'll make it happen."

"Beth?"

"We have to fight. We fight and stop the bastards, or Kripkeni becomes their base for terrorizing the galaxy."

"NT?"

"Whatever it takes."

"Corey?"

"I'm with Beth. We fight here, now, to protect Earth. We win now, or we will be defending Sol from the invaders."

"Janish?"

"The speed of the *Dugr* is an advantage. Can we make strafing runs? Will they be enough to stop the distribution of the weapon?"

"Cass?"

"I think you should ask Bonnie."

Everyone turned their head to Corb's daughter.

Death to All, Bridge

"Commodore, the fighters have opened a hole in the invader's hull. The invader has lost power. It continues to roll, but it no longer has thrust or main engines."

"Captain, move us now! Shields to the maximum."

"Commodore, the fighters?"

Commodore Jexond's reply was calm. "Captain, move us now, or we all die."

The Ajawlil battlecruiser rolled and swung away from the battle. Her engines at flank speed.

All power was lost when the invader's antimatter explosion enveloped the *Death to All*. One engine nacelle ripped from the carrier's fuselage. Systems damage was extensive throughout the vessel. Weapon controls, shields, navigation, life support, artificial gravity were all offline. The emergency lights told the commodore his ship was in a bad way.

"Report?"

"All systems offline."

"The invasion carrier?"

"Unknown?"

"Go look out a portal!"

The security guard dashed off the bridge to the port dining hall then to the starboard dining hall. When he returned, his report was short.

"There are no ships visible."

Hákarl, Bridge

"That's enough. Call off the dogs."

"Admiral?"

"You heard me. Tell the fighters to retreat. They are to use emergency power. I want them away from here. They are authorized to override the fuel flow restrictor. They are to burn at maximum."

The captain turned to the communications officer and pointed. The communications officer typed frantically, made an exaggerated gesture of pushing the send button, then turned back to the Admiral.

The monitors showed the attack fighters

pulling back, heading in-system.

Sixteen lite freighters are lining up for a run at the invading ship.

"Admiral?"

"Sergeant, they volunteered."

"How many?"

"Two per ship. The captain and a pilot. Thirty-two."

"Admiral?"

"Yes, Lieutenant?"

"We have a fighter sitting at our five o'clock."

Josh smiled, knowing the answer before he asked the question. "Open a channel to the fighter."

"Open."

"Captain Reynolds. How are you doing?"

"Admiral, it is all peaches and cream."

"Good to hear. You know, this place is about to get hot. You think Georgia asphalt in August is hot. You ain't seen nothing. I know you are standing in as our wingman, but you need to be gone."

"Admiral, running isn't really a thing I cotton to."

"Understood, but you are missing an important piece of data."

"Yeah?"

"Yeah. We can jump the *Hákarl* out of the blast area. I'd very much like to drink with you tomorrow. I am asking you, Captain, to get gone so we can drink tomorrow."

Captain Reynolds did not respond. The monitors showed his fighter banking away and heading in-system.

"Admiral, look."

"Yes, Sergeant, I see it. Lieutenant, how long to impact?"

"Forty-seven seconds."

"Captain Patterson, the first lite freighter that enters the invader's hull, is your cue. Do not wait for an order."

"Understood."

Captain Mari Patterson had split her console. The console's left side displays the long-range images of the invader and the line of lite freighters on their attack run. The console's right side was one big red icon that would move the *Hákarl* using its star-portal.

Eyeing the big red digital button, Josh smiled. "What did you do?"

Mari's eyes never left the console and the image of the third lite fighter impacting the hull. "I preprogrammed the sequence. I didn't want to break a string. I think they have opened the hull."

Bridge crew, career military, were openly weeping. Every lite freighter impact was two valiant souls lost. The image of the fifth lite freighter enveloped by the hull was the trigger.

"That's it!"

Mari mashed the heel of her palm on the digital button. The *Dugr* jumped to the pre-programmed location but not far enough. Its shields were not at a hundred percent when the concussion from the anti-matter explosion washed over the ship.

"Report."

"Main engines offline. Life support is offline. Shields are offline. Weapons are offline. Art-Grav is offline. The antimatter containment field is at forty percent. The magnetic containment field will run on batteries. Stand by. We have to cut back on emergency life support.

"We need the batteries to maintain the antimatter containment field."

Part Five

Accept the destiny you create.

Plentari, Main Hall

"Madame Negotiator, the story of today's battles will be told for a thousand years."

Ignoring the Saga, the Plentari Supreme leader watched fighter after fighter slam into the invader's hulls. Two battles were raging with hundreds of Plentari warriors giving the ultimate sacrifice.

Fighter after fighter willingly sacrificing themselves by colliding with the invader's hull. Each attack fighter was rupturing its antimatter containment field.

Explosion after explosion until the invading carriers lit up the sky. First one, then the second. Visible to the naked eye from the planet, the Megvesnaith carrier explosions resembled a small star going supernova.

"A thousand years ... Perhaps, Saga. But it will all mean nothing unless Aalborinn is successful."

"Yes, Madame Negotiator."

Death to All, Bridge

"Commodore, we have restarted two engines. We salvage parts from the third to maintain the two functioning engines. Our navigation shields are operable and will support transit. Artificial gravity is at seventy percent and stable. Life support is adequate. All weapons are offline.

"Scans indicate no other ships survived the explosion."

"Is the hyper-tunnel active?"

"We believe it remains functional."

"Commander, we need repairs. Your orders are to keep this ship together until we reach Kripkeni and the repair depot."

"Yes, Commodore. The Ch'en Executive Council is requesting a conference."

"Ignore them. Get us out of this place."

Hákarl, Bridge

Josh is looking at his console and the frozen image of the *Hákarl's* Chief of Maintenance. Josh has a wry smile to accompany his response.

"Chief, you could have saved a lot of words and said we are dead in space."

"Yes, Admiral."

Josh turned to his security detail. You two run down to the armory and break out two combat exo-suits. Pull their radios. Sergeant, you come back here with one radio. Corporal, you go down to the engine room with the second radio."

The security detail did not wait for confirmation. The big men manually slid the doors open and ran off the bridge.

"Captain Patterson, I presume we are

somewhere close to the outer marker, and we are not going anywhere soon. Work with the communications team. We need to let someone know we are still here."

Spinning her chair around, Mari was face-on, looking up to Josh. "Admiral, how did Mister Johnson contact you? Did Jol have something to do with it?"

"Damn, that's right! Captain, come with me."

Surprised, the young captain followed Josh to his ready room. Josh opened a false wall, gave his palm and eye to the bio scanners, opening a vault. Pulling out a device, he set it on the conference table.

"Captain Patterson, this is above need-to-know. The existence of this device is known to about six people. Most of the TC3 Executive Council does not know we have these. Do you understand?"

"Yes, Admiral."

"Call me Josh."

"Call me Mari."

The young captain's green eyes never left the admiral, her smile beaming, her face glowed. Josh was sure they had a moment.

"What does it do?"

"It creates a micro-wormhole for communications. Essentially, it creates a point-to-point tunnel using wormhole technology."

"Well, I'll be dipped. That's kind of useful. Does the Captain know about this?"

"Yes, it is useful. No, the Captain knows there is embedded technology that allows a form of instant communication."

Josh pressed a series of icons and flipped a digital toggle before he spoke.

"Jol?"

"Admiral Turner, it is good to hear your voice."

"Yes, thank you. Are you still connected to the *Dugr*?"

"Yes, but we have not received communication for some time. You will be pleased to know, the Ajawlil battle cruiser *Death to All* destroyed the Megvesnaith ship attempting to invade K'an.

"The Plentari also repelled the Megvesnaith invasion."

"What about Kripkeni? What about the *Dugr*?"

"The *Dugr* reported destroying one Megvesnaith carrier, but a second carrier appeared."

"Son of a ... Okay, here's what I need you to do. Inform the TC3 of our success. Tell the Chancellor we are dead in space and need assistance. They are to order the carrier Jirmina to return and pick us up."

"Understood."

"Jol, stand by."

"Standing by"

Josh pressed a spot on the conference table, opening a console. After a couple of minutes of frantic keying, he looked to Mari but spoke to Jol.

"Jol?"

"Yes, Admiral."

"We have about ten hours of power before we lose containment."

"Understood, I will ensure Chancellor Wilbon understands the situation."

Closing down the communication device, returning it to the vault, sealing the false wall, Josh turned to find Mari standing at the door.

"Yes?"

"I was wondering if you would like to have dinner."

"Captain Patterson, are you asking a superior officer on a date?"

"It sounded that way in my head."

Chuckling, Josh responded.

"Let's get through the next few hours and see what happens. Yes, dinner with you would be genuinely nice. Genuinely nice, indeed."

They heard a loud banging reverberate through the *Hákarl's* infrastructure. Racing to the bridge, Josh was barking orders before he sat in the command chair.

"Report."

"Something hit the hull."

"That is quite obvious. What was it that hit our hull?"

"Unknown."

"Sergeant, give me that radio. Sergeant, you go to the viewing portal in the crew's mess. Captain Patterson, you do the same in the officer's mess. Look around. Don't miss anything, then get back up here."

They were heading out before Josh finished his sentence. Keying the radio, Josh had an idea.

"Corporal... What is the Corporal's name?"

"Marconi."

"Thanks, Lieutenant. Corporal Marconi, come in."

"I am here, Sarge."

"Corporal Marconi, this is Admiral Turner. I want you to head down to the main bay. Go to the viewing portal on the second level. Run down the catwalk and lookout. Tell me what you see."

"Aye, aye, Admiral."

The security sergeant raced back onto the bridge.

"Nothing but stars."

Mari raced back in time to hear the sergeant's report.

"Nope. Nothing. Stars."

"Corporal Marconi?"

The winded Corporal Marconi responded. "Arriving now. Admiral, there is a fighter to our aft."

"A fighter, is it one of ours?"

"Yes, sir. It looks like it smashed its nose when it hit us. It is dipping its wings, sort of side-to-side."

"Corporal Marconi, stand by. Do not move."

"Standing by."

Holding out the radio toward Mari, Josh asked an honest question. "How do I switch this to the flight combat channel?"

Mari takes the radio and hands it to the communications officer. The communications lieutenant presses a few of the small icons and hands it back to the Admiral. "You are on both channels now."

"Fighter on my butt, your mother says you are none too bright."

"Do you know my mother, Admiral? That does sound like something she'd say."

"We are a little busy here, you know, trying to stay alive. Did you bang into my ship? That dent will hurt the resale value. What is it you want, Captain Reynolds?"

"I figured if you opened that big ass door, I might park this thing on your deck. I reckon I got enough power left to get back to the station in a couple of days, or we could use a power-coupling from my ship to yours and feed the containment field.

"But if you don't want to, I'll be heading out."

"Corporal Marconi?"

"Yes, Admiral?"

"Run and find the Chief. Tell him to open the main hanger outer door."

"Roger that."

"Captain Reynolds?"

"Yes, Admiral?"

"Bring yourself and that bottle to my ready room."

"Bottle, sir? There's no bottle. Besides, I am sure an Admiral, such as yourself, has a much nicer bottle somewhere on his fancy ship."

"Captain, technically, this isn't my ship, but I will look around. Captain Patterson, you collect Captain Reynolds and escort him to my ready room. Sergeant, you join us."

"Admiral?"

"Yes, Lieutenant?"

"The chief says they can't open the outer doors. They are unable to create the vacuum needed to release the pressure on the doors."

"Sergeant, put Corporal Marconi in a full exo-suit. Have him go to the emergency escape hatch on the port side of the main hold. He is to clamp his boots to the deck. Magnets *and* clamps. Both or he will get sucked out through the emergency escape hatch.

"When the main hold atmo evacuates, he can release his boots and use the manual override to open the doors."

"Yes, Admiral."

***Dugr*, Bridge**

"That kuk did not come from the secondary hyper-tunnel."

"No, Ragnar, that blighter dick did not come through the hyper-tunnel. Were they hiding? Why did our scans not find a FULL-SIZED CARRIER with HUNDREDS OF FIGHTERS?"

Lucinda ensured the team stayed focused. "Nick, calm down. We know one thing with certainty. Kripkeni is their primary target. Plentari was a secondary goal, a nice to have. Everything they have done has been a diversion to get that big son-of-a-bitch close to the planet Kripkeni.

"Corb?"

"There is no way a ship that big could have bypassed all the sensors. It is not possible unless they had help. I think this confirms the Megvesnaith have conspired with the Ch'en and probably the Xjaal to subsume the Garune and probably the Plentari.

"Ka'n and Earth were tertiary targets.

"Landry project the possible flight path of that big son of a gun. Where did it come from, and where is it going?"

A red line appeared to the rear of the invading behemoth, indicating the invading carrier's probable flight path along with its origin.

A green line appeared and intersected with the planet Kripkeni.

"We know where they are going. Where did it come from?"

The monitor began a quick zoom, tracing along the red line and the projected route of the Megvesnaith carrier. The zooming stopped on the outer edge of a star system.

Nick was shaking his head side-to-side, forcing Corb to ask. "Where is it, Nick?"

"It is Zerain. There's your answer. That big bastard knew the *Death to All* had departed. They circled back through Zerain. The Xjaal somehow failed to report seeing an invasion fleet. How did they hide from the Ajawlil on Zerain?"

Nick answered his question. "Those Xjaal bastards ... That big boy didn't come through the hyper-tunnels because it would have set off the sensor grid.

"They have been crossing open space for weeks, maybe months."

Lucinda pulled the crew back to the present.

"So, what? We know where they came from and that the Xjaal and Ch'en cut a deal. Again. How are we going to defend the Garune?"

"*We* are not. I am."

Lucinda conceded. "Bonnie, this is your show. Tell us what you want."

"Lucinda, show me high altitude images of the planet. Images of the planet opposite the space stations."

"Landry?"

A six by five matrix of images of Kripkeni Five appear on the monitors.

"No. Are there more?"

A new image matrix appears.

"That one, three across, four down."

The image designated by Bonnie fills the screen.

"That is where we need to be. The invaders are going to attack from the left. We need to be in a position so I can stop them."

Skeptical, Lucinda gently queried. "That makes sense. They want the space stations intact. Why take Kripkeni and destroy the value. Infect the planet. Let the fighters raid and create havoc. Wear down the enemy until they have lost the will to fight.

"Bonnie, what are you going to do? What do you need us to do?"

"Lucinda, the name Kripkeni translates to 'We fight.' They will never surrender. The Megvesnaith are here for the stations. Shipbuilding. They want the ship factories and repair depots."

"You did not answer my question."

Bonnie deflected and began asking questions. "Landry, how long before the carrier reaches the Kripkeni atmosphere's exosphere?"

"Assuming no change in velocity or course,

approximately seventeen hours."

"Landry, where are you in breaking the Megvesnaith communications?"

"I have broken their encryption. I have access to the invader's main computer. However, there is nothing useful. The data was wiped."

Beth interrupted with a statement hiding a question. "They are starting over."

Cass answered the unasked question. "Yes and no. There is no indication the Megvesnaith culture recorded their history. They exist in the moment and for the next raid. But, Landry, if you can access their computer, can you destroy or stop the ship?"

"No, Cass. The main computer is isolated from all other systems. I suspect all major systems are independent of each other."

"Cass, it does not matter."

"What do you mean? Bonnie, what are you not telling us?"

"The Garune fighters will begin arriving soon. They will fight until they are all gone. We will move in and destroy the attacker."

"How? How are we ... How are you going to destroy the attacker?"

"Beth, I do not know. Yet. That image of Kripkeni Five. Landry, what is the population of the landmasses we see? What is the population of the image, extending to the horizon?"

"May I rephrase your question?"

"Yes."

"What is the population in the image projected?"

"Yes."

"Working ... Approximately one point one-five billion."

"Landry, are the stations directly opposite the projected image?"

"Yes."

"Is the orbit of the stations geosynchronous?"

"Yes."

Cass's tone was soft. "Holy shit ..."

Lucinda was annoyed she had not yet comprehended Bonnie's intent. "Yep, I do not like the new Cass. I liked it better when you were sweet and kind and did not swear. I am blaming Ragnar."

"Guilty."

"Bonnie, would you care to tell the rest of us what you and potty mouth have planned?"

Bonnie pauses, thoughtful.

Under the stars,
she will stand to face her destiny.
Under the stars,
hers is a destiny to create.
From above,
she rains death.

"I always understood the death in the story

to be the Megvesnaith. But I see it now ... Yes, this is the place. Nick, can you put us close to the location in the image?"

"Yes, but that is close to the planet."

"Landry, how far?"

"Approximately two-hundred thousand kilometers from the planet."

Bonnie continued, focused, and determined. "How far from the exosphere is the projected position?"

"Approximately eighty thousand kilometers."

Weeping for the death,
her friends rejoice.
Mercy and pain are her companions.
From above,
she rains death.

"Bonnie?"

"Yes, I was thinking. Lucinda, if we attack now before they get to the planet, we may destroy the invaders, but we will destroy Kripkeni Five also. The shipyards and the repair depots will be taken offline for decades. Landry, show the blast radius of an antimatter containment breach on the invading carrier."

The image clearly showed the significant population centers and the orbiting stations taking the brunt of the blast.

"We wait until they get into the exosphere on this side of the planet. The thermosphere will deflect the blast around the planet and out into space."

Corey whined. "Bonnie, it will kill all those people."

"Yes, it will. Landry, what is the entire population of Kripkeni Five, including the shipyards?"

"Seven point seven-five billion people."

Mercy is naught.
She does not turn away from her pain.

"One point one or seven-point seven?"

Corey looked away.

Bonnie's tone is increasingly more firm. "Lucinda, it is the only plan."

"Bonnie, what is your plan to rupture the magnetic containment field?"

Under the stars,
she will not look away.

"I will pull it apart."

Corb's tone indicated concern. "How are you going to do that? Can you do that?"

"Yes, I can do it."

Corb's tone is of genuine curiosity. "Is that how you knew about the trilateral domain? You can see the domains. It is how you knew to use the three parts?"

"Yes."

"Do you think you can initiate the trilateral slipstream without the symbols?"

"Maybe."

Turning to Lucinda, Corb approved his daughter's vague plan. "I believe she can do it."

Turning to Bonnie, with a sadness, Lucinda's question confirmed the *Dugr's* fate. "What do you need from us?"

From friends at her back,
she will draw strength.

"You have to get me close enough to pull it apart. I may need the *Dugr* to fly toward the invading carrier's antimatter containment field."

Lucinda hemmed before asking. "How close?"

"Does it matter?"

"No, Nick, it does not."

Mercy and pain are her companions.

"Lucinda, what about the fighters?"

"Good question, Ragnar. Landry, get the Supreme War Committee on a conference."

Lucinda laid out the plan to save Kripkeni Five from the invaders. The Supreme War

Committee balked and argued until Corb intervened.

"You will accept our decision. You will deploy every ship with a gun in defense of your planet. Every fighter *will* engage the invaders, or we will depart immediately.

"You know who I am. I am The Redeemer. Before you respond, ask yourself: When has The Redeemer not lived to his word?"

The conference muted, the Supreme War Committee quickly debated before returning to the screen.

"Redeemer, we ask for more time..."

Weeping and rejoicing,
she is of two souls.

Bonnie waved her hand. The spokesperson for the Supreme War Committee grabbed his head and fell forward. Dead. "Enough talking. You will send your ships to protect the *Dugr* in the coming battle. If you do not, we will leave you to become slaves of the invaders. Are there any more questions?"

"We have no more questions. We are issuing the orders now."

The image returned to stars and the approaching invasion carrier.

A long, cold, melancholy stillness fell over the crew. Lucinda softly issued the orders. "Record your logs. Write your goodbyes. Wrap up everything you can think of, everything you feel is essential. Landry, I want you to bundle up the personal logs and the ship's logs. Encrypt the bundle and send it to Jol through Q'eqchi. Michelle and Davinder will know how to retrieve the data.

"We are going to meet back here in two hours."

"Landry?"

"Yes, Lucinda?"

"Can you save your consciousness? Can you send it for safekeeping?"

"No, Lucinda, that is not possible. Parts of my consciousness might survive, but it would be like the reboot we gave Jol."

"Landry, I am sorry. I thought maybe they could get a new cube for you."

"There is no need. I have lived a good life with good friends. This day was inevitable, and I would not want to be anywhere else."

Tears hampered the crew as they are leaving the bridge.

Bonnie sat, thinking.

From friends at her back,
she will draw strength.

Dugr, Bridge

"We are at the extreme edge of the

exosphere. Bonnie, does this look right?"

"Yes, Nick, thank you. Lucinda. Can we spin the ship? Put the main hold outer doors toward the planet?"

"Yes. Why?"

"Landry, can we open the outer bay doors and maintain atmo?"

"Yes, the atmo shielding will allow you to stand on the deck with the outer doors open."

"Little Bit, why do you want to do that?"

"Uncle Nick, I want a real, unobstructed view."

Under the stars,
she will stand to face her destiny.

"The Garune fighters are returning and engaging the invaders. They are taking out the invaders almost five to one, but it is not enough."

Lucinda continued to mentor her prodigy. "Beth, order them to fall back and defend the *Dugr.*"

"Order them?"

"Yes, tell Landry to put you on their command channel and order them to defend the *Dugr.* Remind them if the *Dugr* falls, Kripkeni Five will fall."

"Landry?"

"You are connected."

"This is Captain Davies of the TC3 attack

vessel *Dugr*. Your new orders are to disengage and fall back to our position. Priority is to defend the *Dugr*. All other priorities are rescinded.

"Failure to defend the *Dugr* in its battle with the approaching invasion carrier will result in the capture of Kripkeni Five by the Megvesnaith.

"Repeating, this is Captain Davies of the TC3 attack vessel *Dugr*. Your new orders are to disengage and fall back to our position. Priority is to defend the *Dugr*, all other priorities rescinded."

"Comms closed."

"Thank you, Landry. Do you think it worked?"

"The squadron commanders are asking the Supreme War Council for instructions. Stand by … They have new orders to defend the *Dugr*."

Lucinda was struggling to control her voice. "Bonnie, what do you need from us?"

"Captain?"

"Yes, Landry?"

"The invasion carrier is accelerating. Recalling the fighters appears to have gotten their attention. They have not changed course. ETA to exosphere fifty-one minutes."

"Thank you. Bonnie, what do you need from us?"

From friends at her back,
she will draw strength.

"If you can keep the *Dugr* together until I am able to rupture the containment field. That would be swell."

Realizing Bonnie was trying to be humorous in an understated way, Nick chimed.

"Yeah, it would be neat if those Garune fighters had help. Ragnar, JJ, can you guys shoot the little guns at the midges? Cass, a spot of tea would be lovely."

"Get your own damned tea."

"Wow. Relax, Cass. Ragnar, remind me again what you see in her?"

"Besides beautiful and smarter than hell, she's not afraid to tell you off."

"Too true, and that is gorgeous."

Weeping for the death,
her friends rejoice.

"Bonnie?"

"Yes, Dad?"

"Whatever happens, you stay focused on pulling apart the containment field. Even if we destroy the carrier, the contaminant will not be destroyed if we don't create the antimatter explosion. It will drift through the atmosphere and infect the planet."

"I am aware."

Corey cleared his throat. "I have meant to ask ... Now seems like a good time. The contaminant, I know they use blood as the transport to distribute the biological agent, but what, exactly, is it?"

Cass responded. "It is a neurotoxin that creates a trance-like state. It is similar to, but much more powerful, than the Pufferfish Tetrodotoxin used by the Voodoo Priests of the Caribbean."

"Zombies? It creates zombies?"

"Essentially, yes, but more like compliant slaves."

"Captain Davies?"

Raising an eyebrow and getting an okay from Lucinda, Beth responded. "Yes, Landry?"

"The Garune fighters have encircled the *Dugr*. You may want to order them to create an opening between the *Dugr* and the planet."

"Why would I do that?"

"Because I need an unobstructed view of the invading carrier?"

"Right. Sorry, Bonnie. Landry, can you help?"

"Yes."

"Then send the message from me."

Immediately the fighters begin to create an opening between the *Dugr* and the planet.

"Landry?"

"Yes, Captain Davies?"

"There is only one captain on this ship."

Lucinda smiled at her mentee.

"Understood."

Bonnie understood the verbal interplay.

Corb called the team to the line.

"Nick, don't let the *Dugr* move."

"No movement. Got it."

"Ragnar, JJ, no fighters get close."

"Roger that."

JJ nodded.

"Beth, Cass, NT, keep her in one piece as long as possible."

Nods and tears confirmed they heard the instructions.

"Bonnie, Lucinda, Janish, let's head down to the hold. Landry, open the main hold outer doors."

"Corb, what about me?"

"Corey, do whatever Beth tells you to do."

Dugr, **Main Hold**

Bonnie is standing two meters from the invisible shielding that keeps the atmosphere in the main hold stable. Directly behind, Corb stood, looking over his shorter daughter. To his left, Janish, his right Lucinda. The Triad at her back gave Bonnie a sense of ease and calm.

They know we cannot escape the blast.
They know we are going to disintegrate
into atoms.
They stand here, now, my friends.

From friends at her back,
she will draw strength.

I can feel them.
They are powerful.
The Triad.
For them, I must not fail.

Under the stars,
she will not look away.
From above,
she rains death.

"Here she comes."

Bonnie raises her arms parallel to the deck, palms forward. She feels the Triad, holding hands, pushing energy to her.

She is pulling strength from the Triad.

Pushing her hands forward, she stops with her palms as wide as her shoulders. Pointed toward the slow-moving carrier, she begins to pull.

She can feel the energy and power surging. She begins to wave her hands slightly. In, out. In, out. She is destabilizing the invasion carrier's antimatter containment field. She can see and feel the magnetic restraint vibrating.

***Dugr*, Bridge**

Landry's artificial voice is calm. "Beth, the attacking fighters are attempting to destroy the *Dugr*."

"Are they attempting to ram us?"

"Yes, I believe those are their orders."

"Ragnar?"

"We got this, but a little help from Landry might not hurt."

"What? Landry, can you help?"

"Yes, in self-defense, I can take over fire control, but Ragnar and JJ have to pull the triggers."

"Do it!"

"The self-defense laser turrets drop then reposition when the Landry AI subroutine takes over."

"Wow, like shooting fish in a barrel."

Beth is disgusted. "No, Corey, those are people we are killing."

Ragnar and JJ focused on their targets. The fire control algorithms do not miss. The space around the *Dugr* is filling with Megvesnaith attack fighter debris.

The symbols on the riser begin to glow. "Landry, split the main monitor. Put the main hold on the right. What are they doing?"

***Dugr*, Main Hold**

"I can't get it. They are rerouting power to the magnetic containment field. Dad?"

"Bunny, focus. Stay focused."

Corb tugs Janish and Lucinda a step closer to his daughter. Sensing the need to push harder, Janish raises her left hand toward Bonnie's left shoulder. Lucinda does the same on the right.

Bonnie feels the power from the Triad surging, tingling, growing.

"Keep doing that."

***Dugr*, Bridge**

The symbols grew too bright, too quickly, causing the crew to scramble. Cass began pulling on Ragnar's goggles. Beth was helping Nick. Corey was waved away by JJ, who pulled on his goggles while maintaining fire on the attacking fighters.

The monitor image of the main hold fades to black.

"Landry, where are they? Get them back?"

"Beth, they are still in the main hold. The electromagnetic interference is blanking the imaging sensors."

"Compensate."

"Apologies, Captain, I am unable to compensate. The imaging sensors have a failsafe to protect from massive amounts of radiation."

Dugr, Main Hold

"There! That! Keep doing that!"

Bonnie felt the cracks form in the containment field. In her mind's eye, she envisioned the rupture. Occurring in one-billionth of a second, she was able to see the magnetic containment fracture with her focus.

Turning her palms outward, with her outstretched arms, she spread the expanding particles of death away from the *Dugr*.

The explosion was expanding in all directions. Slowly widening her hands, the invisible growing death bending around the *Dugr*.

Dugr, Bridge

The external cameras, sensors, lights, and viewing monitors simultaneously reacted to the explosive flash by going dark across the ship. Consoles, monitors, and sensors are rebooting from failsafe protocols. The red glow of the emergency lighting felt like death to the crew.

The riser symbol's glow stopped in an instant. The lights are flickering back on, and the artificial gravity was stabilizing. Beth is shocked to be alive.

"What the hell happened?"

"Beth, I am putting shields to maximum."
"Landry?"
"Beth, the Megvesnaith carrier has been destroyed. Nick, we need to move away. The residual radiation is lethal."

Nick pressed the icons for the emergency jump controls. The main hold outer doors slam closed. The *Dugr* re-appeared two-point-two lightyears above the elliptical plane.

Dugr, Medical Bay

Nick had moved the *Dugr* to a safe distance quickly, but the few seconds of delay was too long for Aalborinn and the Triad. Her hands dropping, Corb leaned forward to grab his unconscious daughter before she fell to the deck. He teleported his daughter to the medical bay. Laying her on the examination bed, she opened her eyes when Corb allows the mechanical arm to administer an injection.

From above,
she rains death.

"I did it?"
"Yes."
"Are we okay?"

"I don't know."

Dugr, Main Hold

Watching Corb save his daughter, Lucinda reached across to grab Janish's elbow. Janish stumbled toward Lucinda, who tugged at her life-long friend, the immense pressure is tearing at their connection. Lucinda held up the small waif, knowing they were in trouble. Janish had teleported herself and Lucinda hundreds of times. Lucinda wondered if this would be the last time.

Arriving in the medical bay several seconds after Corb, they were already showing the signs.

Dugr, Medical Bay

"Landry?"

"Yes, Corb?"

"Help Lucinda and Janish."

"Ladies, please lay down. I am going to administer the compound."

Helping Janish onto an examination table, then lying down herself, Lucinda never stopped confirming facts. "Compound?"

"Yes, it has a potassium iodine base with the new elements we received from the Ch'en."

"Will it work?"

Landry does not respond.

She weeps for the dead and rejoices at life.

"Dad, I couldn't hold it any longer. When my hands dropped ... When my hands dropped, the radiation hit us."

"Bunny, today, you saved billions. If the Megvesnaith had conquered the Garune, how many more billions would fall into slavery?"

Looking across to Janish and Lucinda, Bonnie sees they are not conscious. The mechanical arm swung around from Janish to inject Corb with the compound.

"When my hands dropped ... They were no longer protected. Dad, I couldn't protect them."

"What was the line in the story? Yes, I remember. 'Weeping for the death, her friends rejoice.' We are here, and we do that which is required. We always have. It is who we are, and it is all we ever wanted from our lives. Lucinda and Janish loved you more than life itself. Do not weep for the loss. Rejoice in friends so powerful they stand with you to face the future."

"Landry?"

"Yes, Aalborinn?

"Are they going to be okay?"

Landry deflects.

"Corb, Aalborinn, please remain still. You require additional medication."

Dugr, Galley

Nick and NT stopped taking their meals with the crew. For ten days, the individual isolation of loss washed over the *Dugr*. The grief is overwhelming.

Beth is the *Dugr's* de facto Captain.

Aalborinn, whose dark curly hair is now soft brown, had not spoken to anyone since the day of the incident. Beth is trying to get the crew to respond and prepare to depart.

"We will be home in four days."

Corey is unable to control his irritable tone. "Beth, how can you know that? Can we initiate the slipstream?"

"Corey, I can initiate the slipstream and maintain it for as long as needed."

Beth is skeptical. "Bonnie, are you sure?"

"Beth, my name is Aalborinn. I will be known as Aalborinn, Daughter of the Redeemer, First Daughter of the Plentari. Yes, I am sure.

"JJ, do you want us to drop you at Plentari before we head to Sol?"

"Aalborinn, I am happy to take a transport from Earth to Plentari. I know returning to your home is important."

"That is kind of you, but we will stop at Plentari. I wish to see the Madame Negotiator."

"Very well."

"Beth, I will speak to my father, Nick, and

NT. We should be ready to go in a couple of hours."

Not waiting for a reply, Aalborinn leaves the galley.

Dugr, Nick's Cabin

"Little Bit, I know it was not your fault."

"Uncle Nick, please come talk to us. We need you. We are going home."

"Home, that will take forever without the Triad and the slipstream."

"I can initiate the slipstream. Father and I can maintain it indefinitely. I have an idea about that. What if I can tie the navigation console into the symbols to control the wave?"

Nick stared, thinking. Thinking long enough that he realized it was the first time in ten days, his mind was not absorbed with memories of Janish. Aalborinn sat unmoving, waiting.

"Thank you. I needed that."

"No, thank you for giving us your greatest love."

Weeping for the death,
her friends rejoice.

Through their tears, Nick hugged the woman he called Little Bit before she departed.

Dugr, NT's Cabin

"NT, I do not know how to help you."

"I don't need help, Bonnie. I need time. I will be okay. Not today. Not tomorrow. One day, I will be okay."

"What are you going to do?"

"Do? I am going to retire. She left me her family's ranch in Alberta. I am going to go there and live a quiet life."

"You know how to reach me if you need anything. NT, I am serious. If you need anything, just ask."

Mercy is her pain.

Bonnie wiped the older man's tears. The pain of seeing the strong man weep tore a hole in her heart.

Dugr, Corb's Cabin

"Bunny, I am going to be okay. I know you know, but I will say it anyway. In my life, we have done many incredible things. We brought more to Earth than anyone thought possible.

"We never considered death. We always knew it was there, hunting us. He was stalking us. Building allies to take us from our families.

"I expected …

"I did not think we would survive when you

deflected the explosion.

"The Triad could not have done that. As powerful as we were ... We could move ...

"We could not have ruptured the containment field. Bunny, you have ... real power."

Bonnie looked at her father, examining the wrinkles and age she had not seen before.

"Is that why you had Beth falsify the report? To hide my power?"

"Yes. We will report the facts, the truth, directly to your mother and Davinder. Classified reports leak. We want people to think we got in a lucky shot.

"The little white lie will protect you."

"What about the Garune? They know what happened."

"No, they know what we told them. The explosion destroyed everything in the blast radius. Everything except the *Dugr*."

"What does it mean?"

"It means you have a destiny. Only you can determine what your destiny is, or how to find your future."

"What am I going to do?"

"I am going to talk to your mother. I think you and Beth will make a powerful team. But we will talk more later."

"Destiny. Nona told me the Wilbon women are strong and powerful. For Nona. For mother. For you ... I will search for my destiny."

Under the stars,
she will not look away.

Aalborinn kisses her father's cheek before leaving. Using his nanobots, Corb begins the transition.

"Landry?"

"Yes, Corb."

"Transfer the ownership of the Dugr."

"Before I initiate the process, do you want any changes to the documents you prepared?"

"No, leave them as they are, send them, but keep it low-key."

"Corb, it will not be a secret."

"True, but we do not have to advertise."

"Corb, with ownership of the Dugr, Bonnie will become a target."

"Her name is Aalborinn, and she is already a target."

Dugr, Bridge

"Helm?"

"Captain Davies, we are good to go."

"It is good to have you back, Nick."

"It is good to be back. Look at me taking orders from a girl whose nappies I used to change. Life does make you wonder."

Smiling, Beth turned to Aalborinn. Corb in his chair on the riser. Beth in the command chair. Aalborinn in the third chair atop the riser.

"How fast do you want to enter?"

"No need, please put on your goggles. NT, work with Landry. Let's figure out a way to mute the light these symbols emit. I don't want to wear these damned goggles."

NT's single nod confirmed he was thinking about the request. When everyone donned their goggles, Aalborinn turned to Beth.

"Beth?"

"Let's blow this pop stand."

Aalborinn closed her eyes, and the symbols erupted with a bright light. Tinged with a blue hue, everyone knew the glow was different, more powerful. The *Dugr* leapt into the trilateral domain.

Aalborinn spoke with her eyes closed. "Nick, you should be able to control the wave through the new interfaces."

"Right-O. I see the controls. Where did these come from?"

"Landry and I created them.

"Landry, make sure your new algorithms are accurate."

"Yes, Aalborinn."

"Landry, are we traveling that fast?"

"Yes. Nick, check your console."

"Well, damn. Isn't that just tickety boo?"

Epilogue

Geneva, A Nice Restaurant

"No, Corey, there is no us. There is no future where I see us together. The academy allowed one break in the training. I chose to visit my mother here in Geneva. We were nineteen and full of hormones. You were a second-year Cadet in a fancy uniform. Please stop pestering me and move on."

Realizing he has made a mistake. Corey puts money on the table and walks away. He does not understand. No restaurant in Geneva, or anywhere, will allow Aalborinn to pay for anything.

The savior of the galaxy has an open table everywhere. Sipping her wine, she is enjoying the warm evening.

He is too weak.
I need someone strong.
I need to find out about the Index and the place called Rýma.
Lucinda said Landry could revive in a new cube.
Where are the cubes?
Rýma?
Cass will know.
I will visit Cass and Ragnar.

Alva must be eleven or twelve by now.

Mercy is naught.
She does not turn away from her pain.

The Index and Rýma are the keys.
Landry and Jol, they will know something.

TC3, Head Office Building

"Come in."

Captain Mari Patterson is wearing an orange summer dress designed to contrast with her green eyes.

"Wow. Uh. I mean ... It was you. At that first graduation. Captain Patterson, what are you doing here?"

"Yes, that was me. I am glad you remembered. I spoke to Michelle and General McCaffey. Your orders are to stop working and take me to dinner."

"You called General McCaffey? At the Pentagon?"

"I sure did and told him that I was going to take you to dinner, and he insisted on you taking some R&R."

"Mari ... Are you sure?"

"Typical man. Come on. I made a reservation."

Geneva, A Nice Restaurant

Aalborinn sees Josh and Mari walk in. Waving them over, they see Corb's bright eyes and radiant smile in his daughter.

"I will leave you two to your evening, but first, can we chat?"

Mari is beaming. Josh is nervous and quiet.

"Mari, how would you like to pilot the *Dugr*?"

"What? Are you kidding? I mean, hell yeah."

"Aalborinn? That is not yet public information."

"Josh, come on. Tell her."

"It is not final ... Mari, Beth has been given command of the *Dugr*."

"Can you do that? Can the TC3 do that? The *Dugr* is not, technically, TC3 property."

"Yes, *technically*, the *Dugr* belongs to Corb.

"Michelle, Davinder, and I spoke to Corb. He is, uh, leasing it to the TC3. Leasing it for a specific purpose."

Josh stopped and turned to Aalborinn.

"*Technically, Dugr* belongs to me."

"Yes, it does."

"Mari, we have to talk to the Ch'en. Those bastards know something, and I want to know what it is. Also, I need to convince them that their impression of me is mistaken."

"Impression of you?"

"The Ch'en consider me to be an abnormality. I am not human under the Ch'en ethos. Which, of course, is their way of trying to build allies against me. They resent being indebted to me."

"Why are they indebted to you?"

"It seems I was able to ... Never mind that now ... Mari, what is it, Nick says? 'There's never any bullshit. We are running forward, eyes closed, going to get a whole lot of dead but, what the hell, we will figure it out.'"

"Sounds like fun to me."

The trio clinked their wine glasses at Mari's accepting the new role.

"I have to visit the little boy's room. You two chat. I will be right back."

When Josh is out of hearing distance, Aalborinn is beaming. She leans in and whispers. "Josh? Really? Going big time. Good for you."

"What can I say."

They tip their glasses and smile. Aalborinn speaks very softly.

"What do you know about the indexes and where they came from, the hidden planet?"

"Indexes? Hidden planet? Nothing."

"Come on, think back. Did anyone mention anything? Where we, where Cass, might have gotten all that information?"

"No, not that I can remember. But, wow, I'm in. Tell me more."

"My father told me there is more. We need to talk to the Ch'en, help them get their mind right, then find the hidden planet."

Aalborinn's nanobots interrupt her thoughts. "Aalborinn?"

"Yes, Landry?"

"You are being observed."

"Observed by whom?"

"Corey."

Looking around, she sees Corey striding toward their table. A gun pointed at her head. Putting up her hands, she speaks to the few other diners. All of whom are TC3 security operatives with their sidearms pulled.

"Relax, he is simply confused. Corey put down the gun. We can talk this through."

"No. No, we cannot talk. You never talk. You give orders. You did all this. TC3 is letting me go, and the Air Force is discharging me. You did this. I have nothing. You did this."

Exiting the men's room, Josh is working his way around, behind, Corey. Aalborinn gently puts up a stop sign, Josh stops. Seeing Corey's finger begin to squeeze the trigger, she raises her hand, deflecting the gun upward. The bullet enters the ceiling above Mari.

Before the security teams can fire at the assassin, he crumples to the floor, dead.

Mercy is naught.

Josh saunters back to the table, watching the security team drag away the body. Sitting, he pours himself more wine.

"Will they know it was you?"

"No, he had a cerebral hemorrhage. An abnormality in his brain caused the delusions and eventually burst."

Nodding, Josh continues. "Aalborinn, if you go looking for the answers to your questions, you will find a lot of resistance."

"Answers?"

Ignoring the silly question, Josh tells Aalborinn what she needed to know to confirm her destiny.

"Start with Cass. No, first, get your mother and Davinder to sign off. No one is going to talk to you unless Michelle and Davinder sign off.

"Then talk to Cass and Ragnar. They know everything."

"What about you?"

"What about me?"

"You must know."

"I know what I know and some of what I was told. But I was not there. Beth was there at the end of the Muh'xan conquest. She might know something, but you need Ragnar and Cass. Also, talk to Nick and NT but start with Ragnar and Cass. Cass will know."

"Come on, Josh, I don't believe you don't know more."

"Oh, I know enough. But I am not telling you."

"Why not?"

"Because I have had one good date in three years, and instead of a nice, quiet dinner, we get dead people. Dead people, okay, but I am talking to you about flying off and getting dead WITH MY DATE."

The security details all turn to the raucous laughter erupting ten minutes after someone died.

Aalborinn downs the last of her wine, pushed Corey's money to Mari, and stands to leave. Hugs all around before she is on the sidewalk. Thinking.

Under the stars, hers is destiny to create.

Thank you!

*"Anyone who says they have only one life to live
must not know how to read a book."*
Anonymous

Dear reader, please accept my sincere gratitude for spending your precious time reading the words I was able to patch together. I am often reminded of how lucky I am to write and do more than I ever imagined.

*"O Lord that lends me life,
lend me a heart replete with thankfulness."*
William Shakespeare

I have my health, a loving family, a wonderful wife, and an overwhelming yearning to keep them all.

R. C.

Glossary

Ajawlil (A-jaw-lil) – A race of warrior clones fealty bound to The Redeemer.

Ch'en (Cha-en) – The inhabitants of K'an.

Dugr (Dug-er) - *Dugr* is an old Norse word that translates to Fearless.

Georgie (Georgie) – To annoy Bonnie, whose given-name is Georgina, Jessie names his fighter *Georgie*. A name she hated as a kid.

Hákarl (Hau-K-arl) Originally the Nordic word for shark, today it is the national dish of Iceland consisting of a Greenland shark.

Jaderna (Ja-der-na) – A fierce, powerful, Plentari.

Jadexna (Ja-dex-na) – Younger sister to Jaderna.

Jamoke (jə-ˈmōk) an ordinary, unimpressive, or inept person.

Jirminach (Jer-min-ack) Jirminach (JJ) Johnson is Plentari/Human hybrid.

Jol (J-awl) – An artificial person stationed on the TC3's orbital space platform.

K'an (K-awn) – The closest planet to Earth, linked to Q'eqchi via an interstellar conduit.

Kripkeni (Krip-ken-ee) The home of the Garune people.

Landry (Lan-dree) – An artificial person permanently assigned to the *Dugr*.

Megves Prime (Meg-ves Prime) – The homeworld of the Megvesnaith.

Megvesnaith (Meg-ves-nāth)- The inhabitants of Megves Prime

Muh'xan (Muh-Shan) – Small race of sentients who conspired with the Ch'en and the Xjaal to colonize Earth.

Plentari (Plen-tar-ee) – A matriarchal society, their name is singular and plural. It refers to both the solar system, the planet, and the inhabitants.

Q'eqchi (Kek-chee) – This is the TC3's alternate command center, under the Smokey Mountains of West Virginia.

Rýma (Rye-ma) – This is the name of the hidden planet where Corb and the team found the information and acquired the *Dugr*.

Summitate (Su-mi-tah-te)

- Summitate Potentia: Possess the power to move objects with a form of telekinesis.
- Summitate Medicina-Aspicios: Have both the ability to heal wounds and to perform a form of remote viewing.
- Summitate Rationalis: Enjoy increased mental abilities. The gift of Summitate Rationalis improves the ability to think in a coherent approach, with superior cognition, and at a remarkable speed.

Xjaal (Xha-awl) – A race of clones designed to perform administration.

Xunantunich (Xhu-nan-tu-nich) – Is a Mayan temple in the Belize mountains, which is Earth's terminus for the interstellar conduit to K'an.

About R. C.

Fortunately, in secondary school, my interest in reading was sparked. A close friend and an instructor who took an interest in a boy he later called 'The rebel without a clue.' were instrumental in learning the value of a good book. Both piqued my interest in reading.

My lifelong friend inspired me to read J.R.R. Tolkien, and I became addicted to the fantasy genre. The instructor required me to read exciting historical novels for academic credit. Frank Norris, Leon Uris, and Ken Follett are inspirations and fuel my love of history.

Born to a military family, it was logical that I follow the military tradition. However, after four years of "yes sirs" and scraping the wax off floors, I decided there must be more fun in a corporate career.

After thirty-plus years of work experience across the globe, the corporate career landed me in Colorado.

Contact R. C.

Website
www.rcducantlin.com

Facebook
www.facebook.com/rcducantlin

Twitter
twitter.com/rcducantlin

LinkedIn
www.linkedin.com/in/rcducantlin

Books by R. C.

Novels

Summitate Series
Biomass
Dominion
Connections

The Plan: Create A Pandemic. Use A Designer Drug To Cure The Flu And Kill Six Billion People. Hope For Humankind Fell On Me To Control The New Humans.

The Carina Series
Time is an Illusion
A Calm Mind
Our Place
BairnGefa
Ho' Ma' Utz

The Blessing Of Interstellar Travel Has Become A Curse. With The Powers He Received from the Designer Drug, Corb Has One Chance To Save Earth, But It Has Become Impossible To Tell Friend From Foe.

Aalborinn
The Reluctant First
The Girl of Light
Ka'i: The Second First

To Become A Plentari Warrior: Survive The Brutal

Training. Can Corb's Daughter, A Human Girl, Become A Plentari Warrior? How Many Will She Slay To Survive? Is She The First?

Short Stories

MAX AND THE DREAM TIME
THE FIND
THE EVERWHEN
THE TONTINE
THE LOST YEARS
THE PRICE OF LOVE

Jamie's future will break Max's heart. Understanding the Orb becomes Max's obsession. With the Orb, he can make sure the future he sees never happen. Can His Friends Save Him From the Pain? Will Their Plan Work? Is The Pain Too Great To Endure?

MIRANDA EVERLASTING
GRIS-GRIS
FÒ MIRANDA
ENVIE

Young Miranda is going to be famous. She is going to be in the movies and fly aeroplanes. The dreams of children destroyed, Albee helps Miranda become famous.

Not all voodoo is bad voodoo.
Some voodoo is for the dead.
Some Voodoo Is For The Living.

Voodoo Is Eternal.

AYDIN TRAMMELL
PTARMIGAN LANE
MANDARIN PITH
SHINY LIES
DESIGNER SHACKLES
SALT WOUNDS

2021
FUTURE SILENCE
DIMENSIONAL BOUNDARIES
UNDERSTATED REALITY
LIVING WITH MIRRORS
BROKEN ECHOES

A former Special Ops Commando thought covert missions in the desert were rough. Then he married a spy who wants him dead.

When Aydin Trammel becomes an international intelligence operative, he quickly learns his new career is considerably more complicated than when he was a special ops soldier. Back then, problems were solved more straightforwardly: Hike in, blow something up, hike out. He was good at that.